THE COLONEL'S MONOGRAPH

WARHAMMER™
HORROR

WARHAMMER™
HORROR

THE COLONEL'S MONOGRAPH

GRAHAM McNEILL

WARHAMMER HORROR
A BLACK LIBRARY IMPRINT

First published in Great Britain in 2019 by
Black Library,
Games Workshop Ltd.,
Willow Road,
Nottingham, NG7 2WS, UK.

10 9 8 7 6 5 4 3 2 1

Produced by Games Workshop in Nottingham.
Cover illustration by Miklós Ligeti.

See Warhammer Horror on the internet at

blacklibrary.com

Find out more about Games Workshop
and the worlds of Warhammer at

games-workshop.com

Printed and bound by CPI Group (UK) Ltd, Croydon, CR0 4YY

---

*To Nick and the rest of the Black Library crew for keeping the candle
burning at my dusty scrivener's desk these last few years.*

WARHAMMER™
HORROR

A dark bell tolls in the abyss.

It echoes across cold and unforgiving worlds, mourning
the fate of humanity. Terror has been unleashed, and
every foul creature of the night haunts the shadows.
There is naught but evil here. Alien monstrosities drift
in tomblike vessels. Watching. Waiting. Ravenous.
Baleful magicks whisper in gloom-shrouded forests,
spectres scuttle across disquiet minds. From the depths
of the void to the blood-soaked earth, diabolic horrors
stalk the endless night to feast upon unworthy souls.

Abandon hope. Do not trust to faith. Sacrifices burn
on pyres of madness, rotting corpses stir in unquiet
graves. Daemonic abominations leer with rictus
grins and stare into the eyes of the accursed. And the
Ruinous Gods, with indifference, look on.

This is a time of reckoning, where every mortal soul
is at the mercy of the things that lurk in the dark.
This is the night eternal, the province of monsters
and daemons. This is Warhammer Horror. None shall
escape damnation.

And so, the bell tolls on.

My name is Teresina Sullo, and these will be my last words.

This is not hyperbole, nor do I intend for you to read them as melodramatic, for I abhor exaggeration when more often than not, truth is drama enough.

I am reclusive by choice, and in my long life have made only a very few close friends. Those generous souls I am fortunate enough to count as such, together with my late husband, would describe me as a venerable woman of quiet reflection, sober judgement and principled methodology. It can safely be said that I am a private person, not normally given to outpourings of emotion.

I want you to hold to that as you read further.

This record exists only so that no matter what slanders

may be aired upon the occasion of my death, you will understand the truth of the matter.

Though I suspect you will not thank me for that truth.

I write by candlelight within the walls of the Cardophian Repository, which is to be found within Servadac Magna, the sector capital of Yervaunt. Presently, I sit at an ink-stained desk in the office of the Archivist Primaris, a position I was privileged to hold for three decades until my retirement.

If you are unaware of the Cardophian Repository, allow me to briefly illuminate you. It is a venerable institution that has occupied its present site for the last four millennia, established in the last year of M36 to preserve the history of our world and its surrounding subsectors. Its grand structure is a much-lauded example of post-Akkadian Gothic, and boasts many fine collections of early Imperial histories, Ecclesiarchical art and, regrettably in light of current circumstances, an irreplaceable collection of pre-Apostasy illuminated manuscripts.

But I digress – an inveterate habit of mine, which I must now attempt to curb as there is little time left to me, and I fear my resolve may falter if I delay overmuch. Thus, dear reader, with my bona fides and distaste for inflammatory rhetoric established, please believe me when I make the following statement:

I encountered true evil at Grayloc Manor.

To any who knew me, it ought to have come as no surprise that I accepted Garrett Grayloc's invitation to catalogue his late mother's collection of antiquarian books.[1] I was, of course, familiar with the colonel's patronage, what with her many donations, though I had only ever dealt with her factotum, and had never met the woman in person.

Her beneficence had resulted in fevered speculation among my staff as to what other books and esoterica the colonel might keep, for her private collection was rumoured to be extensive and comprised of volumes of such antiquity that simply to touch them would result in their complete disintegration. I discouraged such talk, but my acceptance of her son's request was driven in no small part by my own curiosity. You will, no doubt, be aware of the many idioms dedicated to the downfalls such sentiment inspires!

Devotion to work has been my lodestar for as long as I can remember, a guiding light, set in the firmament of my being by the Emperor, blessed be His name. This devotion has weathered all that time and life has placed in my path, even the terrible events that later transpired at Grayloc Manor.

It is this devotion that brings me back to the repository tonight.

I had been gainfully employed by the Cardophian Repository in one capacity or another for over a century. Taken on as a scrivener's inker at age thirteen, I diligently and

---

[1]   Colonel Elena Grayloc of the 83rd Yervaunt Voltigeurs (a light regiment of the Astra Militarum with a long and storied history of heroic actions in this sector and beyond) was well known as a collector of artefacts on the campaign trail, many of which she subsequently gifted to the Cardophian Repository prior to her death.

methodically worked my way up through the archival hierarchies of academia – as vicious (if not as bloody) as any battlefield in the neighbouring Ocyllaria subsector – to reach the lofty rank of Archivist Primaris.

Under my supervision, dedicated teams of archivists, lexicographers and data-miners shouldered the burden of a historiographical establishment of the means by which the great campaigns of Lord Militant General Hexior Padira III would be recorded. Twenty-six years after the completion of that work, our labours were rewarded with an honoured footnote in *A History of the Later Imperial Crusades* – a matter of considerable pride to all of us.

In time, I would lead efforts to archive the sermons of Cardinal Saloma.[2] This, in particular, was a thankless task, given the aged prelate's penchant for never committing anything to paper or slate from that campaign, and the paucity of corroborating records following the humidity crisis of the Great Ingress.

But, as had become increasingly clear to me over the decades, Imperial archiving is a task for the young and fortitudinous. My health had begun to suffer from many years of breathing in fixative particulates and preservative chemicals, and the surgeries effected upon my lungs were only partially successful in undoing the years of damage.

And as debates about various methodologies of archiving continued to rage between the conservatory factions,

---

2   Cardinal Saloma was a hero to the people of Yervaunt after she led an army of the faithful alongside the 83rd Yervaunt Voltigeurs against the forces of the Archenemy in the latter years of the forty-first millennium.

it was decided by those with no appreciation for the importance of things like mass deacidification or print permanence that it was time for me to finally put aside my quill and hang up my frictionless proxy-gloves.

With one hundred and thirty years of life behind me, and an unknown number ahead of me, I was retired from my post. I received full honours, and a statue with a passable resemblance to me was erected in one of the moderately traversed galleries. My husband thought it made me look severe, but I saw only devotion in the sculptor's craft and was much taken with its likeness.

Though I at first resented this enforced retirement, I quickly took to the more leisurely pace of life, and found time to read purely for pleasure, without the need for cross-checking, data-sorting and fastidious indexing. The simple joy of a well-told story became my pleasure as I rediscovered the works of dramaturges like Philaken, Gorso and Shakespire.

Though I was no longer employed by the repository, I nevertheless consulted with its archivists on a regular basis, for my expertise still had value. Many of this world's nobility sought out my discerning eye to establish the veracity and value of their family's heirlooms, Imperial Charters and genealogical writs.

Retirement was treating me well until the day Teodoro died.

I had recently returned from the long and tiring task of systemising the database of criminal records in the nearby port city of Hesarid. It had been a weeks-long endeavour that allowed for the proper cross-referencing of various evidentiary records and resulted in the perpetrators of seventy-six unsolved murders finally being brought to justice.

The day after I returned to Servadac Magna, I said goodnight to Teodoro, and retired for the evening, leaving him reclining in his favourite chair by the window with his first edition of *The Spheres of Longing*.

When I awoke the next morning, I was alone, and made my way downstairs to our parlour. There, I found him still sitting in his chair, with the book open on his lap. Tears streaming down my cheeks, I pulled a chair next to his and finished the verses he had been reading. I had loved my Teodoro from the moment I first met him, and now he was gone, I felt a yawning emptiness in my heart.

The medicae later told me Teodoro had suffered a ruptured brain aneurysm, causing a subarachnoid haemorrhage that likely killed him before he even knew it was happening.

He did not suffer, which is the only consolation I was able to take.

The weeks following his death are grey and empty to me, as though the records of that time were consumed by waves of grief as caustic as the radioactive storms said to have erased the ancient library of Neo-Aleksandrya. I can recall little from that time save for the condolences and support of friends, which I am sure were welcome, but could do nothing to heal the void within my soul.

Into this void arrived Garrett Grayloc's petition in a monogrammed envelope of vellum embossed with his family crest; a Tetrarch Prince from a regicide set.

The letter within was succinct, the handwriting uneven and alternating between left and right leaning, not the neatly kerned and leaded script of a scrivener servitor. I was impressed by the personal touch, even if the new master of Grayloc Manor wrote with a brusque tone that could be interpreted as somewhat condescending. At this time, I did not know if Garrett Grayloc had served in the Astra Militarum, but clearly a measure of the mother's military mien had passed to the son.

I have not the time to reproduce the full letter, but in summary, it requested I travel south to Vansen Falls and present myself at Grayloc Manor, where I would assist with the cataloguing of the late colonel's library. Together with a generous fee, a groundcar would be placed at my disposal as well as whatever else might be necessary for the swift completion of the work.

Like a drowning sailor clutching a lifeline as they sink for what they know will be the last time, I seized the opportunity. I wanted to lose myself in work, to devote myself to my craft so thoroughly that it would numb the grief I was feeling.

I immediately drafted my acceptance.

The following morning, a groundcar was waiting for me: a Kiehlen 580 from the previous century. I had travelled enough in my years to appreciate the comfort and craft of fine engineering, and this was just such a vehicle. The interior was deep red, of a soft leather that would make the seven-hour journey south to Vansen Falls far more tolerable.

The driver was a brutish and, thankfully, mute

servitor-chauffeur, which alleviated the need to engage in small talk, an activity I abhor and with which I have little skill. Spared the need to communicate, I opted to spend the journey reading what little information I had been able to gather concerning the late Colonel Gray-loc and her family.

But soon after leaving the outskirts of Servadac Magna proper, the landscape took on a curious quality I had not previously experienced, and I found myself unable to concentrate fully on my research. I had often trav-elled the environs of the city with Teodoro, and we had delighted in the untamed splendour of the landscape. Now it seemed altogether more desolate and threaten-ing, as though nature were on the verge of reclaiming what humans had taken for themselves.

Each time I returned to my reading, I was troubled by the feeling of an unwholesome gaze upon me, a sense of being appraised in an altogether predatory manner. In my youth, I was more often aware of this sensation, as are the majority of my sex, and though it had been some time since I had known such scrutiny, the feel-ing was instantly recognisable. In the end, I put aside my papers, and simply concentrated all my awareness on my surroundings.

The ground grew steadily higher as the Kiehlen left the tamed flatlands of the interior and climbed towards the wilder coastal mountains. Farther out from the city, weed-choked ruins pressed close against the cracked and curving highway, while the encroaching forests pressed looming shadows over the glass of the ground-car's windows. Red bracken and rust-gorse spread beyond the treeline like spilled blood, and the few agri-collectives I saw appeared singularly barren, with a uniform aspect of dilapidation clinging to the pre-fabbed dormitory blocks and silos within.

When a rise in the road brought the mountains into view above the deep woods, my strange feeling of unease was only heightened. The slopes were too bleak and their summits too lofty, as though they had been deliberately raised to such heights as to keep their secrets hidden from all but the most determined seeker.

Numerous gorges and ravines cut the landscape of our route, and the ancient iron bridges always seemed too rusted and neglected for my liking. The road dipped again, becoming a rockcrete causeway traversing a light-less stretch of mist-shrouded marshland to which I took an immediate and instinctive dislike. Frothed indus-trial scum lay upon the surface of the marsh, and I wondered what secrets might lie hidden beneath its brackish waters.

At some point in this long crossing, the sway of the groundcar, coupled with the oppressive gloom of this stretch of the journey, lulled me into a fitful doze. I am a light sleeper at the best of times, and insomnia has been my constant companion since I entered my eleventh decade, but something in the uniform bleak-ness of these surroundings dragged me down into sleep. Whether it was the nagging thought of unwholesome things hidden beneath the marsh or my already height-ened unease, I do not know, but the dream that bled into my consciousness was of a tenor I had rarely expe-rienced before.

I have no memory of sleep claiming me. One instant I was looking out over the marsh, the next I was deep in the dream. Even as I recall the details now, the fear still sets a cold hand in the pit of my stomach.

It began slowly, almost pleasantly; a sensation of drifting downwards into darkness. This was not threatening, rather it was welcome, like drawing a favourite blanket tight on a cold night. Then the quality of the darkness *shifted*, and what was once comforting became threatening. Enclosing. Suffocating.

...cloying wetness forced into my throat. Paralysing cold sliding over my limbs. Pinning me in place.

...heavy weight pressed upon me. White linen fabric at my neck. Tightening. Choking.

...a voice whispering in my ear. Obscenities.

...icy fingers reaching into my chest. Closing upon my heart.

*...**let me in**...*

I woke with a start, slumped against the car door and unable to draw breath. I tried to speak, but the air was locked in my lungs. My heart raced. No words would come. Paralysis still held me in its grip.

I could only stare at the burnished metallic curve of the servitor-chauffeur's skull.

Slowly it began to rotate on its spinal axis.

I felt the desperate urge to flee, like an animal caught in a hunter's snare.

I could not bear to see the servitor's face. I knew it would be terrible. The ravaged features of a drowned man vomited back into the sunlight after years in the foetid darkness below. Its flesh would be like jelly, bloated and rank with decay, the eyes devoured by sightless things of the swamp in spite for their exile to the inky blackness below.

But it was none of those things.

It was Teodoro, smiling at me.

'Let me in,' he said.

And then I awoke, *truly* awoke.

Only with great difficulty was I able to control my breathing and reassure myself that I had not woken from one nightmare into another. Eventually, I convinced myself I was no longer dreaming, but for the hour it took to complete the crossing of the marsh, I kept my attention fixed on the groundcar's interior. The leather texture of my seat, the gleam of chrome on a door handle, the throb of the powerful engine, the rumble of tires on the road.

Anything to keep my gaze from wandering to the dreadful view beyond the glass.

As the Kiehlen climbed back into the wooded hills, I allowed myself a measure of relief, but it was to be short-lived as the coastal mountains reared up so darkly and precipitously that they seemed ready to fall and crush me beneath their immensity.

Clearly the dream in the marsh was still crawling within my skin!

It had made me susceptible to dangerous leaps of imagination, so I took a series of deep breaths and recited my favourite catechisms from the *Imperator Beneficio*.

The journey to Grayloc Manor was greatly unsettling me, but the comforting words of the *Beneficio* calmed me as they always do. As I have previously set down, I consider myself a rational woman, not given to flights of fancy, but this journey was filling my head with ill thoughts and dark imaginings.

The road then passed into a sheer-sided valley, and the temperature within the Kiehlen dropped so sharply that, with great reluctance, I was forced to instruct the servitor-chauffeur to engage the vehicle's thermal generator. Eventually, after an interminably long descent through the cold valley, the enclosing rock opened up and I beheld the dramatic vista of the western ocean spreading to the far horizon.

The road looped steadily downhill until we crossed a narrow bridge of black steel to enter a coastal township of such charm and beauty that it all but took my breath away, after the maudlin character of the journey.

This was Vansen Falls, and it sprawled pleasantly on the inner slopes of what had once been an impact crater blasted in the planet's bedrock over ten thousand years ago. The rising of the ocean and its erosive powers had collapsed the western portion of the crater wall, allowing water to rush in and form an almost perfectly circular bay, with two jutting promontories to the north and south. An Imperial temple of black stone, hewn from the surrounding mountains, sat precipitously on the northernmost promontory, its spire curiously crooked and stark against the pale blue of the sky.

Across from the temple, on the opposite promontory, was Grayloc Manor.

My first impression was of astonishment, for the dwelling was far larger and more ornamented than I had expected for a soldier. In my years archiving the records of the cardinal and lord militant general, I have had the opportunity to converse with many who served the Imperium as warriors, and even the most senior of those never lived so grandly.

As if in contrast to the temple opposite, Grayloc Manor was primarily constructed from white marble, with flashes of colour worked into its domes and the long magenta banners hanging between its fluted pillars. The high portico of its entrance was grander than many Imperial shrines, and spreading out from the well-manicured gardens were expansive vineyards that tumbled to the shoreline in waves of undulant greenery. Gilded follies, like ornamented birdcages, dotted the slopes overlooking the sea, and I immediately pictured myself seated within one, reading *The Brothers Carmassi* while sipping a sugared tisane.

The little I had been able to learn of Colonel Grayloc, on the journey to Vansen Falls, spoke simply of meritorious service in campaigns fought throughout the neighbouring Ocyllaria subsector, but the sources were maddeningly light on details. She had been awarded the Honorifica Imperialis, but I could find no specific citation. She had been granted leave to retire with full honours, and again I found no explanation of why so senior and capable an officer would be allowed to withdraw from the battlefield at a time when the threat was so great.

Wars against the Archenemy had been raging throughout the Ocyllaria subsector since before my birth. I had never known a time without war, or without the sons and daughters of our world being tithed for the Astra

Militarum. Each time I saw the transports climbing to the bulk carriers in orbit I felt a strange mixture of emotions: guilt and sadness that Teodoro and I had chosen not to have children who might serve the Emperor, yet also relief that we would never send them off to die on some far-flung battlefield.

The groundcar purred smoothly through Vansen Falls, allowing me a closer look at the town itself. Its stone and timber structures spoke of a period of human habitation that predated the Imperium, and the people I saw on its streets were tall, clean-limbed and healthy. Their eyes followed the Kiehlen as it swept past.

The road curved up and around the southern peninsula, and soon the tires crunched on the gravel driveway of the pale house as we came to a halt before its main entrance, an imposing double door of pale blue timber. The servitor-chauffeur disengaged the drive mechanism and got out to open the door for me. I did not look at it for fear of what I might see. The memory of my dream in the marsh was still fresh in my mind. My limbs were stiff from so long in the back of the car, so I was grateful to finally stretch my legs.

The view was quite spectacular, and a path of embossed paviors led a weaving path down the stepped slopes. The crash of booming waves upon the cliffs drifted up to me, and I took a deep breath, tasting chill air freighted with a faint salty tang. I also smelled fresh-turned earth, and the ever-so-slightly acidic tang of the offshore Mechanicus geocore platforms that marred the horizon with a faint petrochemical haze. I turned as I heard the doors opening behind me.

A man in his middle years wearing a crisp tunic-suit of pressed white linen descended the steps to greet me, his hand extended. I had never met him, but the resemblance to his mother, the colonel, removed all doubt as to his identity.

'Mistress Sullo,' he said. 'Welcome to Grayloc Manor.'

Garrett Grayloc pre-empted the servitor-chauffeur's efforts to bring my few bags within, and hefted them with the casual ease of a man not used to others waiting hand and foot upon him. I had, as was my habit, travelled light, but to see the lord of Grayloc Manor bearing my travel cases within his home immediately created a favourable impression of the man.

He set down my luggage, and I took a moment to look around.

The vestibule was high-ceilinged with a curving stone staircase leading to the upper levels and a number of arches leading into other rooms. To my left was a receiving room with white sheets draped across the few remaining pieces of furniture, while to my right was an expansive ballroom large enough to host hundreds of guests with ease. Like the receiving room, its furniture was also draped with white sheets.

The structure of Grayloc Manor was very fine indeed, but my initial impression was that it was absent of the usual finery one expects in such a dwelling; the accoutrements of deep history and long centuries of familial acquisition. I was reminded of the time Teodoro and I had been the last guests to leave an isolated hotel in the northern mountains, as its solitary caretaker worked diligently to shut the building up before winter snows closed the roads.

A single portrait hung opposite the main entrance, a large oil painting depicting Colonel Grayloc standing alongside her command vehicle – a Salamander, I believe. The colonel was depicted in her combat uniform, the fabric torn and bloodstained, her boots caked in mud. The bronze of her breastplate was dented by numerous hard-round impacts, and her battered helmet lay broken at her feet. In one hand she held a power sabre, a plasma pistol in the other.

A trooper's lasrifle was slung across her shoulder.

Clearly Elena Grayloc had not been one to avoid the crucible of combat.

As naturalistic as the rest of the painting was, I felt drawn to her patrician face, framed as it was with silver hair that hung loose to her neck. Her expression was aristocratically aloof, yet weary, and her vividly rendered eyes were a rich golden-green that conveyed a sense of her unwavering purpose.

The resemblance between the colonel and her son was striking, though the younger Grayloc's features possessed less of a war-hardened edge to them. His blond hair was thinning at the temples, but he retained an air of youth to him that appeared natural and not the result of a regime of juvenat treatments.

'I hope your journey was without incident, Mistress Sullo,' said Garrett Grayloc.[3]

---

3   Such was Mistress Sullo's reputation for precision in recall that her former colleagues attest that any conversations thus recorded would likely have taken place exactly as set down here. However, in light of her

I struggled to think of how I might convey how disquieting a journey it had been without sounding ridiculous. I did not wish my host to form an adverse impression of my faculties from the outset, so decided to keep what I had felt to myself.

'It passed most uneventfully,' I replied, 'which is exactly what I hope for whenever I travel, Lord Grayloc.'

'Most excellent. Now, uneventful though it was, you must be tired. And please, call me Garrett. My mother was the one who obsessed over rank and title. Thankfully, something I didn't inherit.'

His words were unusually forthright and strangely accented with a curious lilt I could not easily place.

'Is that an off-world accent I hear?' I asked. 'Daranian, perhaps?'

'You have a good ear, Teresina,' he said. 'Oh, do you mind if I call you Teresina?'

'It would seem only fair,' I answered, and he smiled in return.

'I was born on Yervaunt,' he said, 'but grew up on Darania, learning how to manage the family's inter-system trade networks from my father. I had no impulse to join the Guard, much to my mother's disappointment.'

He shrugged, as if realising he had let slip a confidence to a stranger, and smiled again.

'Come, let me show you to your room,' he said. 'Assuming I can find it, that is. I'm still finding my feet around here. It's been decades since I set foot in this house.'

---

subsequent actions, the possibility exists that this missive was penned as a form of exculpatory record.

Garrett moved to retrieve my luggage, only to find the servitor-chauffeur had followed us within, and now held both my bags.

'Ah, yes, I suppose I should let Kyrano attend to your luggage,' he said with an embarrassed smile. 'I believe he knows the layout better than I do.'

'Kyrano?' I said. 'I was given to understand it was normal practice for servitors to be shorn of their past identities.'

'In most cases, yes, but Kyrano here was senior colour guard in the 83rd,' explained Garrett. 'Threw himself on a greenskin bomb to save my mother's life some fifty years ago. Most of his body was destroyed, as well as his brain, but still he never let the regimental standard fall. My mother said his last wish was to continue to serve. *Only in death does duty end*, you know? Throne, but I must have heard that story a thousand times as a boy.'

I nodded, and took a moment to more fully study the servitor.

Its kind are woven so deeply into the Imperium that they have become virtually essential to its continued workings, yet they are all but invisible. That their names are erased along with their history further pushes them out to the margins, and I wondered then, as I wonder now, what horrors we perpetuate on our own people for the sake of convenience and functionality.

This half human, half cyborgised servitor was bulked out with combat augmetics, but it was clear the individual had been of considerable size even before the Adeptus Mechanicus remade him. Though dressed in smartly functional attire of pale blue tailored silk,

Kyrano looked more like an underhive thug in a borrowed suit. The lower half of his face was obscured, or had been replaced, by a moulded bronze plate that exuded thin wisps of gaseous breath. The remainder of his features were expressionless, one eye having been replaced with what looked like a field-installed augmetic. What little skin remained on his face was pockmarked with what I guessed were shrapnel scars from the bomb that ended his service.

'Perhaps after I have settled into my room, we might reconvene in your mother's library,' I suggested.

Garrett nodded, and I saw relief wash through him. I was reminded that I was only here thanks to the death of his mother. Clearly a complex play of emotions existed between son and mother, though I could not guess how complex at this time. Whatever troubles may rear their head in later life, I am told it is hard to entirely shake the bonds or dysfunctions that grow between parents and their children.

'Yes, of course. I expect you're eager to get to work.'

'Indeed I am,' I said. 'Your mother's collection was a source of great interest to us at the repository, and I would dearly love to see it for myself.'

Garrett gave a shallow bow, and said, 'I hope the room proves comfortable, but instruct Kyrano should anything not be to your satisfaction.'

'Thank you,' I replied, as the servitor began climbing to the upper levels of the house.

I followed Kyrano upstairs, before turning to ask one last question at the turn on the landing.

But Garrett Grayloc had already gone.

Kyrano led me to my room along a series of wood-panelled corridors floored with worn and stained carpets. The notion of a servitor with a name still sat strangely with me, but I was too struck by the air of neglect I saw throughout Grayloc Manor to fully understand just how wrong that was.

We passed a wide set of doors that gleamed with a vivid red lacquer.

'Is that the colonel's library?' I asked.

Kyrano nodded, but did not respond. I wondered if it had the capacity for speech at all.

A little farther along the corridor we reached the room I had been assigned, and I was grateful to close the door behind me and be done with the mute servitor. The chamber was indeed functional, much larger than I had been expecting, but I shall not waste time on its description, save to say that its furnishings had the musty smell common to items having been kept in a basement, an impression only heightened by the folded white sheets piled on a threadbare chaise longue beneath a cracked window with a view of the ocean.

After settling in to my room and taking some time to refresh myself after the journey, I sat at an antique desk and took some time to more fully acquaint myself with the colonel's history from the files upon which I had been unable to concentrate during the journey here.

Colonel Elena Grayloc had commanded Guardsmen for seventy years, earning almost every battle honour it was possible to win and drawing admiration for both her military conduct and intellectual achievements. During her time in the Astra Militarum, she was a prolific writer, composing numerous treatises on regimental tactics and leadership that are still required reading at the Yervaunt schola progenium.

She also became something of a collector, amassing a wealth of rare texts from her many victorious campaigns and shipping them back to the library in Grayloc Manor.

It seemed her star was in the ascendant, with her promotion to the rank of lord militant general or, some whispered, even lord commander of the sector, all but assured.

Then the Archenemy launched a counter-attack that few within high command will openly speak about or even acknowledge. It has since become known as the Dawn of Dark Suns, a night where the stars reportedly went out and the bonds between regiments of the Astra Militarum were sundered as they have not been since the age of the Great Betrayal.

A dearth of reports exist that chronicle the Dark Suns campaign, in part because so few survived it.[4] It is impossible to obtain confirmed casualty figures, but I have heard rumours that over thirty-six million Guardsmen were lost in that one disaster.

Colonel Grayloc had led her soldiers in a fighting retreat that lasted nearly three years of gruelling guerrilla warfare and desperate survival against the odds.

Her regiment, which had started out fifteen thousand strong, finally returned to Imperial space numbering a mere two hundred souls. For her meritorious service,

---

4   Many of the survivors of this benighted campaign were subsequently confined to the lunatic wards of the Hospice of Cardinal Saloma Arisen. As of now, only one yet survives.

Colonel Grayloc was awarded the Honorifica Imperialis, though as I have previously recorded, I can find no specific citation as to the exact circumstances surrounding the action that led to this award. The colonel was granted a discharge with full honours, and retired to her estates on Yervaunt, where she would live out the last fifteen years of her life as a recluse, emerging only rarely to attend regimental functions and low-key philanthropic events.

I checked my chrono and saw that ninety minutes had passed since my arrival.

Gathering the papers spread across the desk, and returning each document and report to its assigned place within my folders, I then rose with a groan as my back twinged painfully. The chirurgeon has told me often enough that sitting too long at a desk is not good for me – an occupational hazard of the archivist – so I began a series of stretches.

As I worked through exercises to loosen the muscular cramps around my vertebra, I took a moment to admire the shrine on the opposite promontory through the window. It was a fine structure, and I resolved to walk around the crater to offer prayers at my earliest opportunity.

Until then, I decided it was time to visit the colonel's library. I pulled my long silver hair back into a ponytail and opened the door to my room.

Kyrano was standing right outside.

The servitor stood motionless, his bulk filling the doorway.

'Throne!' I cried, stepping back.

I was struck by the sudden sense he... *no, not he, it* had been waiting for me.

When I recovered my composure, I said, 'Excuse me, I wish to visit Lord Grayloc's library now.'

The servitor did not move.

I repeated my request, and this time the lens of its right eye whirred and clicked, its iris dilating as if in appraisal. Reluctantly it seemed, the servitor decided it would move. It bowed its head and stepped aside. I closed my door as I moved past it and walked the short distance towards the red lacquered doors.

As I stood before them, all thoughts of how I had admonished my staff for their fevered speculation as to what might lie within Colonel Grayloc's library were entirely forgotten. I felt giddy at the prospect of beginning my work and learning what lay within.

I gripped the handles, took a breath and pushed the doors open.

The library of Grayloc Manor was perhaps smaller than I had expected, but what it lacked in scale, it more than made up for in content. Its high ceiling was vaulted with square coffers, the interiors of which were decorated with repeating patterns of square-cut spirals that drew the eye around the space, no doubt as its architect intended.

Another portrait hung opposite the entrance, this one stiffer and more formal than the one hanging in the vestibule. This depicted Colonel Grayloc, now clad in the rich dress greens of the 83rd Yervaunt Voltigeurs, staring imperiously out of the canvas. She stood beside an archaic map table piled high with scrolls, and with a gilt-edged book tucked in the crook of her arm. The colonel's weapons – the battered lasrifle, plasma pistol and power sabre – were hung on polished wooden plaques beneath the painting. I wondered if they were still functional.

Tearing my gaze from the colonel's visage, the first thing that struck me was the faint smell of age and preservatives, of powders, and the hum of precise temperature controls. Light diffused from the upper skylights with the crisp quality of polarisation, and cast a pleasingly warm illumination. Where the few parts of the house I had recently seen appeared somewhat neglected, no expense had been spared in the library's upkeep.

Elaborately carved walnut shelves lined every wall, rising from floor to ceiling, and each shelf groaned with potential. Books of all ages, dimensions and descriptions were neatly stacked in a pleasing array of colours and sizes, each a portal to knowledge and understanding.

A rush of sensation and memory surged through me; of my youth as an inscriber and conservator of damaged manuscripts, of weeks spent in the basement archives of the repository hunting down one elusive piece of corroboration, and the simple joy of finding a lost book that had been mis-shelved centuries before.

I have been intimately connected with the written word for as long as I can remember, and it has always elicited in me the deepest of emotions. My father taught me to read with his mother's torn and stained copy of the *Imperial Infantryman's Uplifting Primer* (only much later in life did I realise those stains were her blood). Growing up, I learned never to ask for playthings or confectionaries, but my mother would never say no to a new book.

Tears pricked the corners of my eyes, and I exhaled slowly to calm the sudden and unexpected recall of youth.

'It's quite something the first time you see it, isn't it?' said Garrett Grayloc, emerging from the space between two shelves with an armful of books. He set them down perilously close to the edge of the table with a carelessness that set my conservator's soul on edge. I hadn't known he was there, and quickly reasserted a measure of control upon my emotions.

Only now did I notice the collapsible packing crates lying stacked in one corner of the library. A handful had already been assembled, and a quick mental calculation told me there were not nearly enough to contain even a fraction of the library's books.

'It is impressive,' I agreed. 'Is everything here physical?'

'Yes, my mother didn't hold with data-slates, even in the Guard. Claimed if it wasn't set down on paper then it wasn't real. Always hand-wrote everything.'

I moved through the space, resisting the urge to run my fingers down the spines of the books just to feel the texture of cracked leather and gilt binding.

'That will make my job easier,' I said.

'Good, the sooner this is gone the better,' he replied, hefting another armful of books from a nearby shelf. I resisted the urge to tell him to be careful. These were his books, after all.

'Gone?' I said, a flutter of panic welling in my breast. 'I'm not sure I understand.'

Garrett nodded. 'Yes, was my letter not clear on the nature of your engagement?'

'It spoke of a desire to have your mother's collection catalogued,' I said. 'Nothing of the purpose behind that effort was mentioned.'

'Ah, that was remiss of me,' said Garrett, pointing to the stacked crates. 'Just so we are clear from the outset, it is my intention to sell the entire collection.'

'Sell it?' I said, aghast. 'Why?'

Garrett sighed and said, 'My mother possessed many qualities, but sound financial judgement was not one of them. Our family's trade dealings have enjoyed Imperial Charter for over two thousand years, ever since Fydor Grayloc first broke Uglork Splitfang's blockade. Our fortunes have risen and fallen with the tides of war, but we have always maintained a solid fiscal foundation from which to do business. Unfortunately, many of our most lucrative trading partners are in systems now lost to us beyond the Great Rift, and the maintenance of an inter-system fleet of ships is ruinously expensive.'

'This collection is likely priceless...' I said.

'Which is why I wish you to catalogue its contents and place a fair market value upon each volume it contains,' said Garrett. 'It has recently become clear my mother lived far more extravagantly than any of us suspected, and her debts are what might be charitably called calamitous. I had to release what staff remained and begin selling off the furniture to keep the bailiffs from our doors so you might complete your work.'

That surprised me. My admittedly limited knowledge of Colonel Grayloc was that she had lived simply in

Vansen Falls until her recent death (I had, as yet, not read anything that revealed how that end had come). I wondered how she had incurred such catastrophic debt, but refrained from asking so indelicate a question.

'My father has made it clear that he will see everything in this house down to the last nail sold before he liquidates any of our business assets to pay my mother's arrears,' continued Garrett. 'And neither he nor I wish to hold on to reminders of the past.'

I could understand the reality of the situation, but part of me rebelled at the notion of selling so important a collection. The shelves of the house Teodoro and I shared had been replete with books, and the thought of ridding ourselves of any of them, even volumes we knew we would never again read, filled us with horror.

But these were not my books, and all of us have things that connect us to pasts we would be better off letting go. I could not know what bad memories lurked in Garrett's family histories, nor what painful associations his mother's books might have for him. If ridding themselves of these books was what they needed of me, then who was I to judge them for that?

'Very well,' I said. 'I will begin immediately.'

'One last thing. You may be aware that my mother was also something of a writer.'

I nodded, and Garrett continued.

'She mainly wrote military books, but she also contracted with a local printer to publish a few collections of poetry and, if you can believe it, romantic verse. I'm told she even wrote a passably reviewed novel.'

I hadn't known that, and Garrett read my expression.

'I know,' he said, 'it surprised me too.'

'Assuming they are here, do you wish those books set aside?'

'Throne, no!' said Garrett. 'I've no interest in them, but there was one book the staff mentioned that she never published.'

'What was the book?'

'I'm told it was a memoir of sorts,' said Garrett. 'A monograph.'

'A monograph? Do you know the subject?'

'I am given to understand it describes the events that led up to the Dawn of Dark Suns.'

With my task laid out before me, I threw myself into cataloguing the colonel's collection that very night. Garrett Grayloc gave me carte blanche to conduct the work in whatever way I saw fit, so my first week was taken up by systematising a methodology; breaking the effort into genre, author, subject and style, which would allow me to classify each text according to its veracity, age and condition.

Immediately, I saw it would require many weeks if not months to complete this task, but I cared little for the time it would take. Immersing myself in the art of my profession would be intensely satisfying, as it had been too long since I had rolled my sleeves up, snapped on frictionless proxy-gloves and donned an appraiser's loupe.

Each shelf was identified by a numbered ceramic disc set within the shelf edge, but they appeared to be placed at random – or at least I could find no pattern to their placement. For example, shelf sixty was next to shelf three, which was adjacent to eleven and twenty-nine. Each night I sought to work out the system of numbering, to no avail.

If there *was* a sequence, I could not find it.

The collection itself encompassed a wildly varied span of time periods and styles. The bulk of her books were, as was only to be expected, of a military nature. Over the coming weeks, I catalogued no fewer than two hundred copies of *Tactica Imperium*, and ninety-four copies of *The Uplifting Primer*, each with a subtly different bias to their contents, depending on the fighting style of the regiment that printed it.

Equally common were planetary histories of the worlds on which the 83rd had fought, and I grouped these together, reasoning that the more complete each collection, the greater value it would possess. I cross-linked those to other books describing the various regiments and commanders the 83rd had fought alongside. Presumably these had been exchanged between officers in the field, and while some were blatantly hagiographic in nature, they offered fascinating windows into human cultures across the Imperium.

Naturally, most of the military books were concerned with the fighting histories of the Astra Militarum, though a few touched upon the legendary heroes of the Adeptus Astartes. The *Book of Five Spheres* described the dogmatic warfare of the Imperial Fists, while a series of twine-bound pages purported to be one of the sole surviving excerpts of the Prandium Consul's *Codex Astartes*. My favourite of such books was a tome clothed in animal hide and penned by an unnamed warrior of the White Scars: *Hidden Chronicles of the Chogorian Epics.* I kept returning to this book, and such was the skill of the writer that I felt I could taste the wild salt flats of the Chapter's homeworld.

Religious texts were also common, and I collated numerous editions of the sermons of Sebastian Thor and Dolan Chirosius. I even found a mildly heretical volume in the form of a book of catechisms said to have belonged to Cardinal Bucharis before his fall to apostasy. I recorded numerous textbooks as well; legal doctrines mainly. *Corpus Presidium Calixis,* various planetary versions of the *Book of Judgement* as well as books of natural philosophy such as Drusher's *A Complete Taxonomy of Gershom,* Linnaeus' *Nemesis Divina,* and the medico-anatomical texts of Crezia Berschilde.

I also recorded a great many biographies of Imperial heroes. Some, like the individual chronicled in *To Serve the Emperor,* described acts of bravery that were almost beyond belief, while others, like a first edition of Ravenor's *The Mirror of Smoke,* broke my heart anew.

Most of the texts were valuable and of considerable age, dealing primarily with human institutions, which was to be expected in the library of an Imperial hero, but a great enough proportion delved into subjects that were less expected and would no doubt create a stir when listed at auction.

These risqué volumes were mostly concerned with the cultures of xenoforms: *Dogma Omniastra, Greenskins and How to Kill Them, Aeldari Perfidy, Obscurus Analects of Xenoartefacts,* and Locard's seminal *Biophage*

Infestations. The possession of any one of these works might not raise too many eyebrows, but to see so many gathered together was certainly surprising, though I put the colonel's possession of so many texts of this nature down to the maxim of *know thine enemy*.

Frustratingly, the one book I saw no sign of within the library was the colonel's monograph. Any record of the Dawn of Dark Suns would be of incalculable worth, and the completist heart of my archivist's soul longed to study its contents.

What knowledge might it contain? What *secrets?*

I was working on the assumption that the book depicted in the portrait hung at the entrance to the library was the volume I was seeking, reasoning that the colonel would keep such a book close to her person at all times. Its binding bore a specific pattern, a golden circle with a rippling line bisecting it horizontally and a cruciform arrow running through it, parallel to the book's spine. The symbol was unknown to me, yet I felt it held the key to locating the book. I confess, in my eagerness to find the colonel's monograph, I did not stop to consider *why* it might have been hidden.

The system of categorisation (such as it was) that existed within the library did not obviously suggest a section in which I might have found the monograph, but then, I had not expected it to reveal itself so easily.

It would be hidden in a way that would be obvious only to Colonel Grayloc herself.

In lieu of a dead woman's instructions, it was going to require time and patience.

* * *

My nights at Grayloc Manor were restful, and the insomnia that so often plagued me abated almost entirely after a few nights. At first, I put this down to the ocean air or simply exhaustion from spending so long in the hermetic vault of the library.

How naive that now sounds.

For the most part, I did not dream, and modesty forbids me to record in detail those few I *did* have. Suffice to say, they were entirely pleasant memories of intimacy with Teodoro that saw me awaken with my skin sheened in sweat and the breath hot in my throat.

I miss my husband more than I care to describe here, but I pushed thoughts of him to the back of my mind. I was not yet ready to face the full weight of grief, and work was my way of keeping that loss at bay for a time. Perhaps that was cowardly, but each of us face loss in different ways, and this was mine.

Between cataloguing the colonel's books, I began exploring my surroundings.

The grounds of Grayloc Manor were extensive, though much of its grand finery had been overtaken by nature now there were no groundsmen to maintain it. Its best years had passed, but I saw enough to wish that I had known the gardens in full bloom or that it might one day be restored. But, as with all things, every moment of neglect makes any former perfection harder to reclaim.

I discovered a hedge maze with winding pathways overrun by creeping weeds and bracken. The hedges had grown so high and crooked that no cheating was possible, but the decrepitude of age has not withered my recall, and I easily divined the path to its centre.

There I discovered a tall statue wrought from a curious, pinkish material that somewhat resembled coral, yet was smooth and pleasing to the touch. It featured an abstract figure dressed in flowing robes with proportions and features that were curiously ambiguous. From certain angles it resembled a beautiful man, while from others I found it to be a woman of superlative comeliness. Its outline was protean, as though the statue had once been pliant and had settled naturally into this shape, as opposed to being sculpted by chisels and smoothed by rasps. A marble bench that mirrored the curve of the cratered bay partially encircled the statue, and I lost many an afternoon in contemplation of this figure's elusive truth.

No plaque existed to offer clues as to the statue's identity or creator, and when I asked Garrett Grayloc, he told me it was something his mother had brought back from an ocean world of floating cities. Beyond that, he could offer no further clues as to its nature.

Beyond the maze, there was a hexagonal landing platform with the regimental emblem of the 83rd all but obscured by the jetwash of aircraft. It sat next to a small hangar I felt was built perilously close to the edge of the cliff. Peering inside, I saw the hangar was now home to the Kiehlen 580 groundcar that had brought me here. Whatever aircraft the colonel might once have possessed had clearly been sold already.

I took most of my meals upon the sun-dappled patio to the rear of the house or within one of the many vineyard follies. During one mid-afternoon perambulation, I discovered steps running from the lowest of the follies that zigzagged down a precipitously steep cliff to a small jetty artfully concealed in the rocks at its base, though I saw no evidence of a boathouse.

Kyrano served my food, and I gradually became somewhat used to the limping servitor, often throwing out rhetorical questions to it whenever a particularly knotty taxonomic issue presented itself. With no voice or mouth it of course gave me no answers, but the very act of questioning often led me to the answer I sought. I still found myself uneasy whenever it spent any amount of time in my presence, but its strength was a boon when I required heavy crates of books moved.

Of Garrett Grayloc, I saw little, save for on those few occasions he entered the library to enquire as to my progress. He was frequently distracted, which I attributed to dealing with creditors and the settling of his mother's affairs. He would, each time, enquire as to whether or not I had found the monograph, and left disappointed when I answered in the negative.

His tone was always casual, but the tension behind his words was hard to miss. With every question I became more and more convinced Garrett Grayloc already had dark suspicions as to what might be contained within his mother's memoir.

I tried not to speculate what that might be, but I am only human.

Could it be the unabridged story behind her citation for the Honorifica Imperialis?

Perhaps the truth behind the stars going out?

Or something more sinister?

After three weeks of constant work, even I conceded

that a break beyond the bounds of Grayloc Manor was required. As the sun rose on the twenty-second day after my arrival in Vansen Falls, I dressed in a loose-fitting tunic of pale green and pulled on a pair of sturdy walking boots, intending to hike around the rim of the crater to the Imperial shrine.

The wind blew in cold from the ocean.

Rain clouds gathered on the horizon.

I set out early, following the road the Kiehlen had taken through the town. The sun was bright, but low cloud cover rendered the sky washed out like grey dishwater. The air bore the crispness of oncoming winter, but I had a long padded coat that kept me warm as I descended the curve of the crater.

The stiffness in my back had eased a great deal, and there was a vigour to my step I had not felt in a long time. I saw only a few of the town's inhabitants as I entered its outskirts, and though they nodded in greeting, they kept on about their business. I did not find this unusual or rude, for only those with pressing desires were about at this hour.

The buildings of Vansen Falls were old indeed, older even than many in Servadac Magna, and the texture of their walls was gnarled and eroded by salt winds from the ocean. They were, nevertheless, characterful, with no two alike, and a variety of heights and widths that made each one unique.

I had brought my sketchbook, and though my works will never be hung in a gallery, I take great solace in the act of sketching a fine landscape or a handsome building. I saw many buildings I would happily draw, and resolved to take another day to do just that.

The smell of baked bread and fresh-brewed caffeine drew my attention to a quaint, timber-framed eatery built of greenish stone, with rippled-glass windows. A projecting sign named the establishment as Gant's Confectionary and Recaff Emporium. I entered and was delighted to find the interior was just as rustic as the exterior.

'Greetings of the day, ma'am,' said the owner, an aproned man with a ruddy complexion and a welcoming demeanour. 'Zeirath Gant, at your service.'

'Greetings be upon you, sir,' I replied. 'I was on my way to visit the temple on the headland, but the rich aromas from your establishment diverted me.'

The majority of our conversation had no bearing on what was to follow, but when I introduced myself and spoke of my task at Grayloc Manor, Gant's demeanour abruptly changed.

He nodded and said, 'Ah, yes, young Master Grayloc, a terrible business. Lost his mother the same night we lost the temple.'

The significance of his latter remark escaped me at the time.

I still did not know how the colonel had died, but I sensed the soul of a gossip within Mister Gant and suspected he would be all too ready to share what he knew.

'May I ask how the colonel died?'

'A terrible business,' said Gant again. 'A boatman found her body broken on the rocks below her mansion when the storm abated. Poor woman.'

I vaguely recalled friends in Servadac Magna telling me of a brief and intensely powerful storm ravaging the western coasts last month, but I had been adrift in the fog of Teodoro's loss at the time and had cared little for anything beyond my misery.

'The storm?' I asked.

'Indeed. Thunder and lightning such as I have not seen in all my days. Biggest storm to hit the Amethyst Coast in seventy years.'

'Most likely she was taking the air and slipped while too close to the edge…' I said.

He hesitated before answering. 'That's certainly what the local authorities concluded.'

'You don't sound particularly convinced by that. Do you believe foul play was involved?'

'I couldn't possibly say,' replied Gant.

'Throne!' I said with extra drama. 'You don't think she was… *pushed*?'

'I don't know, Mistress Sullo,' said Gant. 'Not the done thing to give air to idle speculation, is it?'

'No, of course not,' I agreed. 'Though the mysterious circumstances surrounding the colonel's death have all the ingredients of grand melodrama performed in the Theatrica Imperialis, don't you think? A devoted Imperial servant potentially murdered under the cover of the biggest storm to hit the region in nearly a century. A grieving son newly returned from off-world.'

'Truth is often stranger than fiction,' he answered.

'How so?' I asked.

Perhaps he sensed the intensity of my interest, for his gossiper's soul would say no more. So I thanked him for the conversation, settled my bill and went on my way. Fortified by a hot mug of caffeine and a sugared pastry that was deliciously sweet, I passed through the centre of the town, where I came upon a single wall of basalt atop a raised plinth.

Upon this wall were inscribed hundreds of names, some dating back thousands of years. I paused to read them, and quickly realised this was not a monument to memorial, but of honour. These were the sons and daughters of Vansen Falls, young men and women who had been called to fight for the Imperium. I did not linger, but simply made the sign of the aquila and bowed to the wall before moving on.

The curve of the bay took longer to circumnavigate than I had expected, and the gradient of the streets made the climb steeper with every step. By the time I reached the windswept promontory I had climbed a considerable distance and three hours had passed, but my limbs were filled with such energy that I felt I might have ascended yet further.

Clearly the sea air was working wonders upon my constitution.

A path of black flagstones crossed the wild grass of the promontory.

At last I beheld my destination.

Now I understood the significance of Mister Gant's remark about the temple.

From the road, en route to Grayloc Manor, the temple had appeared quite normal, but now I was closer I saw it was a ruin. I had thought it constructed of black stone, but that blackness was not the natural quality of any material, rather the effects of searing fire. I approached the building, casting wary glances up at its crooked spire as the wind howled over the headland and a light smirr of rain began to fall. The dark clouds I had seen at daybreak gathered in sullen thunderheads on the horizon, but I could not tell if they were advancing or retreating.

The fire had scorched the masonry to its very bones. Nothing timber remained and the heath surrounding the ruin glistened with reflective motes of coloured glass. The temple had been roofed with steel trusses and stone tiles, less than half of which had survived.

For all intents and purposes, the building's shell was intact, but looking through the yawning portal where only splintered fragments of its doors remained, I saw the interior had been comprehensively gutted. I crossed the threshold, feeling a dank chill seep into my bones. The temperature within the temple was markedly colder than without, so I pulled my long coat tighter about myself.

Smashed timbers littered the interior, pews for the faithful charred to ash and ruin.

Alcoves that once contained reliquaries were now filled with melted wax from votive candles like glistening pools of blood.

Drizzling rain drifted down through the broken roof and wind sighed through the empty window frames. It whistled mournfully around the destroyed temple, and sadness touched me at the thought of this house of worship lying abandoned and forgotten.

That emotion was swiftly replaced by anger as I saw

a blackened statue of the Emperor lying fallen across the altar. The Master of Mankind lay in a pool of light shining through the temple's last remaining window.

The sight so distressed me that I hurried out.

By now the weather had worsened, but even the cold rain and bitter wind was better than remaining in the dark of the temple's ruin. I could not bear to re-enter the temple, so walked a dispirited circle around its perimeter.

On the far gable looking over the endless ocean was a glassaic window. The rest of the temple's windows had been destroyed, but this one had somehow survived. It depicted the Emperor of Mankind atop a burning mountain of Old Earth. His holy primarchs surrounded Him, armoured demigods in crimson, gold and cobalt.

It must have been magnificent in its day, but the fire's heat had warped the glass, distorting the Emperor and the figures around Him. Once they had been glorious and inspirational, but the glass had run molten, twisting their faces into hideous leers and making them monstrous.

I could not bear the sight of them so transformed, and turned away as the sensation of being observed crawled up my neck.

I looked around, but could see no one nearby.

Only when I turned towards Grayloc Manor did I catch sight of my observer.

Standing on the opposite headland, a solitary figure shrouded in white.

Distance and the fine rain drifting in off the ocean hazed the abyss between us. Scraps of damp mist coiled about my ankles as I took a step towards the hooded figure.

Something in the way it held itself made me think it was a woman, but I could not be certain.

The low sun prevented me from seeing a face in the shadows beneath the hood, and some ancient, primal part of me was grateful for the mercy of that.

Its head tilted to the side, like a bird on a branch curiously regarding its next meal.

I felt a chill travel the length of my spine as the angle of its neck passed beyond what any human bones ought to be capable of. I saw the back of its hood was stained red, and lines of crimson bled slowly down the length of its shrouded body as I watched.

I wanted to step back, but a warm sigh brushed across my cheek, like the intimate breath of a loved one. Reaching up, I felt the sensation of callused fingertips slipping down my neck. The feeling traced the line of my collarbone, and my heart beat a little faster. I could not move, and the cold of the promontory faded as a pleasurable warmth spread through my body, tingling along my limbs and into my loins. My lips parted and I let out a shuddering breath as the most potent of my recent dreams surged in my memory.

A voice in my head was telling me to avert my gaze from this woman, but the youthful vigour infusing my body smothered it.

The warmth was too welcome. The memories too powerful.

I closed my eyes and took another step forwards.

'Ma'am!' cried a voice, and my eyes snapped open.

A dizzying sense of vertigo seized me as I looked down and saw my feet were at the very edge of the cliff. But for this shouted warning, I would have stepped into thin air and fallen hundreds of metres to a grave of jagged rocks below.

Just like Colonel Grayloc...

I stumbled back from the edge, and the healing warmth fled from my flesh. The day's cold – hard and piercing – stabbed painfully into my limbs. I turned to face the source of the cry that had undoubtedly saved my life.

A figure, as dark as the one across the bay was light, stood in the doorway of the temple. He was tall, broad of shoulder and powerful, carrying something long and club-like.

The figure took a step from the temple, and the breath eased in my chest as I saw it was a heavyset man dressed in threadbare priestly vestments. The object he carried was no more threatening than an umbrella.

My breathing began to return to normal and I turned back to Grayloc Manor.

The figure was gone.

I struggled to find both my composure and my voice as the preacher came towards me.

'Did you see it?' I said at last.

'Ma'am?'

'The figure across the bay,' I said. 'A figure in white.'

He shook his head, and I could see he thought me quite mad.

'Ma'am,' he said, his voice a mixture of concern and wariness. 'Please, come away from the edge.'

I was only too happy to put greater distance between myself and the sheer drop.

'My thanks, sir,' I said as I set foot on the flagstone

path again. 'The mist confounded me. I fear I would have stepped to my death but for your warning. You have my thanks.'

'I am at your service,' he said with a slight bow. 'I am Father Calidarus, the preacher here. Or at least I was until last month.'

I shook his hand. The skin of his palm was rough, the hand of a worker.

'Teresina Sullo.'

'A pleasure, ma'am,' he said. 'Are you visiting Vansen Falls?'

'I am undertaking some archiving work at Grayloc Manor,' I said, nodding towards the temple. 'Can you tell me what happened here?'

'Ah, yes, a terrible business,' said Calidarus. 'It happened during last month's storm. A bolt of lightning struck the steeple in the middle of the night. The flash started a fire that gutted the temple before anyone could lift a finger to save it.'

'How awful,' I said. 'Will it be rebuilt?'

'In time, yes. We have secured some funds locally, and the diocese is securing donations from neighbouring parishes. All being well, Militarum pioneers will soon arrive to demolish the old structure in readiness for the new.'

'And this happened on the same night Colonel Grayloc died?'

'I believe so, yes,' said Calidarus.

I spoke with Father Calidarus for a little longer, affording my racing heartbeat the opportunity to slow, while learning more of the history pertaining to the temple. None of which is germane to this record so I shall omit it for the sake of brevity. Though, looking at the length of this missive so far, achieving brevity may already be impossible.

My return to Grayloc Manor took considerably less time than my ascent to the temple, and by the time I arrived I had reserves of energy I had not expected. The rain that threatened to fall in waves did not come, but the clouds overhead remained looming and low, a taste of what was in store.

I reached the headland opposite the temple, and paused to look back over the bay.

Strangely, the temple still looked intact. Encroaching night and distance conspired to render it completely normal, as though the lightning had not hollowed it out. Thinking back on that moment, I wonder at how easily we are taken in by the *desire* to see things the way we would wish them, and how wilfully we ignore the reality of what only becomes obvious with the benefit of hindsight.

As I entered the vestibule of the manor, Kyrano was waiting for me with a linen towel.

The material was freshly warmed, and was at first welcoming, but something in the quality of its texture made me curiously reluctant to press it to my face. As I patted my arms and skin dry, Garrett Grayloc descended the stairs.

He smiled to see me and enquired after my time in Vansen Falls.

'It was most instructional,' I said. 'I sampled the sweet

delights of Zeirath Gant's establishment, then visited the temple across the crater.'

'Ah, yes, a terrible business,' he said, and the oddly echoing sentiment, which so closely recalled Gant's earlier remarks, sent a curious frisson over my skin. He seemed distracted, and excused himself with a curt bow of his head.

As he departed, I handed the towel back to Kyrano and said, 'Garrett?'

'Yes?'

'Is there anyone else staying at the manor? A woman perhaps?'

A shadow passed over his features, so swiftly I cannot to this day be certain I saw it.

He shook his head and gave me a bemused smile that was not at all convincing.

'No, Teresina,' he said. 'It's just us.'

I returned to my room and locked the door behind me. The bed had been made and fresh water placed in a ewer on the dresser. Fresh flowers, vividly red-leafed Fireblooms, stood proud in a vase and filled the air with a heady, musky bouquet.

A little too potent for my tastes, but not unpleasant.

The day's excursion had left me tired, though not so much as I had expected. The chill damp of the fine rain still clung to me, so I stripped off and took a warm shower in the adjacent ablutions cubicle, taking the time to wash my hair and massage the cold from my bones. By the time I emerged, the space was filled with warm steam and the mirror opposite was fogged with condensation. Soldiers often speak of the simple pleasure of a warm meal on the campaign trail, but for me there was no greater comfort than a warm shower and the feeling of once again being clean.

Wrapping the towel about myself, I wiped a patch of the mirror clear and began applying a moisturising cream to my face. After a few minutes I leaned in, pleased by what I saw. I was no youngster, but I was still a striking woman, and did not feel aggrieved at what time had wrought upon my features.

But... was I imagining it, or were the crow's feet at the edges of my eyes marginally less pronounced? My fingertips traced the line of my jaw. The skin felt tighter to the bone, taut and vital. I ran a hand through my hair, and my eyes narrowed. During my seventieth year, my hair had swiftly turned from a rich auburn to the silver it is today.

My roots were tinted the faint brown of my youth.

I have never been overly concerned with the visible effects of ageing, but the sight of smoother skin and my natural colour returning was far from unpleasant. I have had only mild juvenat treatments over the years; procedures to maintain bone density, neural regeneration, and transfusions to counteract the natural degeneration of vital tissues, but nothing cosmetic. I did not know how this was possible, but to see an echo of the young woman I had once been was pleasing in a way I can scarcely describe.

My vain contemplation was cut short as I heard the sound of my door closing.

Was there someone in my room?

I eased to the door and pressed my ear to the wood. I could hear nothing save the patter of rain on the window glass and the creaks and groans of an old house settling for the night. Warmth evaporated from my skin, and I shivered as cold air seeped in from the room beyond.

Gingerly, I pressed open the door a few centimetres and peered through the crack into my room. I glimpsed the lace curtains at the window twisting and dancing, blown and billowed by soft wind through the cracked glass. I altered the angle of my head to see that the door to my room was closed. I breathed a sigh of relief.

I knew I was being ridiculous and pushed the door open, stepping boldly into the room.

At first it appeared as though everything was just as I had left it, but that initial impression was soon dispelled.

The damp tunic and undergarments I had left wadded in a bundle on the floor by the bed were gone. Laid on the bed were fresh clothes, but they were not mine.

The fresh-pressed uniform of an Astra Militarum colonel was laid out with the precision of an officer's boatman. A worn battle-jacket of deep green lay next to a pair of faded fatigues and a peaked cap of black and red. Leather boots polished to a mirror finish sat with the toes tucked under the low-hanging bedspread.

A tray of food was set upon the antique desk opposite the bed. A plate of rich, pinkish meat, brightly coloured vegetables, and a cut-crystal decanter of what looked like amasec. I have been vegetarian for most of my life, and the meals Kyrano had served me at Grayloc Manor had respected this.

Why now was I being served rare steak?

Next to the decanter was a worn and tattered book, like something an officer might carry to record their thoughts on the campaign trail. The leather of the spine was cracked as though it had been bent back many times, its pages curling up at the corners.

The cover was a faded red, and bore the monogram *M.R.* in faded gold leaf.

I lifted the book and opened it to a random page.

It was not, as I had first dared hope, the colonel's monograph; rather it was a journal of sorts. I immediately recognised what I was looking at: a plan to organise, categorise and order the collection of books in Colonel Grayloc's library, the first entry of which dated back thirty years at least. I had been preparing plans just like this in the month I had spent here.

I pushed the tray of food away and poured a drink from the decanter. As I had suspected, the liquid within was amasec. A fine vintage, too. I flicked through the book, seeing references to numerous books I had already catalogued. Some were books I had not yet encountered, while yet others were ones that appeared to be in languages I could not read.

I lit the desk lumen as night finally closed in.

Isolated in my little island of buzzing light, I lost myself in the intricacy of the writer's process. His handwriting was meticulous (the tone and style of writing made me reasonably confident the author was a man), the methodology impeccable, and his singular devotion to the task at hand reminded me of my own perfectionism.

Much of the journal was given over to a detailed account of the colonel's collection, though alongside the lists of books were occasional annotations by the author on its very nature. Most of these were simple observations on the rarity of certain tomes, but others could be read as admonishments to the colonel for even possessing them. The tone of these observations ranged from simple remarks to commentary that would likely have earned a stern rebuke had the colonel read them.

Had the colonel seen them?

Was that why *M.R.* was no longer the curator of this collection?

Some of his notes I could well understand, for as I have mentioned, more than a few of the books were of a questionable nature. Around the halfway point through the journal, I noticed a distinct change in the tenor of the notes, coinciding with the arrival of a book or books that featured more than once in *M.R.*'s notes.

Its name appeared variously as *The Elegy of Valgaast*, *Lament of Valgaast*, and also *Valgaast Theogonies*, though I could not be certain if these were three separate books or a single volume, given that each title appeared to have been sourced from a different planet and every title appeared to be a translation of the same root words.

I had not seen any of these works, nor any reference to what the name might mean.

Whatever its truth, the book or books had clearly upset *M.R.* to a degree I found hard to fathom. Matters were complicated by the fact that it was clear his mind was unravelling the deeper into the book I went.

M.R.'s handwriting, which had been neat and even at the start, was now ragged and spidery by the time I reached the journal's midpoint. I saw smudged blots on the page (the writer's quill too laden with ink) and frequent scratched-out words. As I drew to its end, more than a few pages had been ripped out, and much of what *M.R.* wrote was virtually illegible.

One portion I *could* read appeared to make reference to the destruction of the temple, while another hinted at a scandalous memoir I could only imagine was the monograph Garrett had spoken of. I found several trembling notes that spoke in terror of something known as the *Inamorata*, though, like Valgaast, no hint was given as to what that might be.

By now, the moon had passed its zenith, and my eyes were heavy from peering too long at the handwriting of a very disturbed individual. It had been many years since I had worked this long into the night, and though some trace of the youthful vigour I had felt earlier today remained, I knew I would be fit for nothing come the dawn were I to deny myself at least a few hours of sleep. I moved the Militarum uniform onto the chaise longue, next to the piled linen sheets. Resolving to query Garrett on why such clothing had been laid out for me, I climbed into bed.

I hoped I might dream of Teodoro again.

I did not dream of my late husband.

But so deep and swift was my descent into sleep that I can recall little of how my dreaming began. I vaguely recall a sense of comfort, of being enfolded in warmth, like a babe in arms swaddled in a favourite blanket. Tight and binding, holding me safe and protected.

But that tightness soon passed from comforting to constricting.

I struggled against the sensation, but I couldn't move. Something was pressing against my face. I tried to move, to roll over, thinking I was still dreaming. I tried to draw breath, but what felt like a heavy cloth was pulled tight over my mouth.

I smelled stale, shuttered rooms and the dry mustiness of age-stiffened fabric.

I tasted dust and dead flowers.

My eyes flickered open as it penetrated my consciousness that this was no dream. I saw only dull whiteness, the thick warp and weft of coarse linen.

A shroud...

I tried to sit up, to push the sheet from my face. My legs and arms were pinned in place, bound tight with more of the rough fabric. It chafed my ankles and wrists as the cloth pulled tighter against my face.

Somewhere, a light bloomed, stuttering and weak; the desk lumen. It silhouetted a heavyset form just beyond the suffocating cloth, its outline blurry and indistinct. I tried to scream, but a wadded bolus of moist cloth forced itself down my throat like a hungry snake.

I gagged, fighting for breath.

Greyness hazed the edges of my vision.

*...**let me in**...*

My chest heaved, desperate for air, but there was none to be had.

I felt rough hands at my neck, callused flesh and

metal. Thrashing on the bed, my body spasmed in fear and desperation. I couldn't breathe, I couldn't move.

And then the choking blockage was withdrawn. My back arched as I drew in a breath that felt like fire in my lungs. The greyness retreated from my vision.

I felt the vice grip on my extremities release.

Frantic, I kicked out and reached up to tear the cloth from my face. I scrambled up the bed as my vision adjusted. Hot, acidic fear surged up from my stomach.

Kyrano stood at the edge of the bed, holding twisted sheets of white linen cloth like a garrotte. They clung to him like the toga of a planetary senator or the king of some pre-Imperial feral world.

His immobile face gave no hint of murderous intent, but in the flickering light of the desk lumen his face was daemonic. Sick with loathing and fear, I frantically pushed myself away.

I fell from the opposite side of the bed, gashing my head on the corner of the dresser beside it. Warm blood ran down the side of my face as I lay, stunned, on the floor. I heard the servitor's heavy footsteps as he circled the bed, moving towards me.

Panic seized me, and I tried to pull myself up, but my limbs were dead weight, numb from their constriction. Instead, I crawled frantically beneath the bed, clawing my way forwards with my fingernails until I emerged on the other side.

My mind was clearing, and my legs ached as blood flowed back to my feet.

I could already feel bruising swelling my wrists and ankles.

Pushing myself upright, I stumbled weakly towards the open door. The corridor beyond was lit by the pale light of the moon. I lurched along its length to where Garrett Grayloc's room was located.

I paused at a turn in the corridor to see if I was being pursued.

I whimpered in fear as Kyrano stepped through my door, pulling rumpled sheets of linen from himself as though tearing free of a cocoon. Our gaze met, but I saw only the bland horror of a dispassionate murderer who barely even notices his victim.

But instead of following me, the hulking servitor turned and walked in the opposite direction, as though he had accomplished whatever it was he had set out to do.

I waited, breathless, at the turn as he disappeared into the darkness of the house.

Tears streaming down my face, I slid down the wall and wept.

The following day, I told Garrett Grayloc everything that had transpired during the night.

'Are you sure he was *attacking* you?' he asked as he poured me a hot cup of herbal tea.

I could scarcely believe he was asking me that.

'Perfectly sure,' I replied, holding out my wrists and leaning my head back.

Garrett drew in a breath as he saw how bruised and grazed both were.

'Damned peculiar behaviour,' he said, taking a seat at the dining room table. 'Perhaps he's stuck in a service loop.'

'A service loop? What are you talking about?' I said, the anger at my assault still burning hot in my chest. 'He tried to *kill* me!'

'Of course I see how you might think that,' said Garrett, holding his hands aloft as he saw my eyes widen. 'Wait, hear me out, Teresina. You said one of my mother's uniforms was laid out on the bed, yes?'

I nodded, too furious to speak.

'And there was a meal of rare steak and amasec on the desk?'

I nodded again as Garrett ran a hand across his chin.

'I think I see what happened,' he said. 'Kyrano's always been a bit glitchy, but it's got worse since my mother passed. You see, and I realise now that it might have been a trifle inappropriate, but you're actually sleeping in my mother's room.'

I could barely believe what he was saying.

'I'm sleeping in your *dead mother's room*?' I said, struggling to keep my tone even.

'Well, it seemed like the most expedient solution, given that it hadn't yet been closed up, though I see now that was somewhat foolish. I apologise for that.'

I should have turned and walked away right there and then. I should have immediately marched down into Vansen Falls and arranged passage back to Servadac Magna.

But I did not, and I still wonder at how easily I was convinced to remain.

Taking my silence as consent to continue speaking, Garrett said, 'So I wonder if perhaps Kyrano was confused, and thought my mother was, well, not dead. Hence the meal and the clothes.'

'I've been here nearly a month,' I pointed out. 'Surely he must have known I was not her?'

'One would think so, but who *really* knows what goes on in the mind of a servitor? The machine-spirit moves in mysterious ways within its servants, after all. Now, I think what happened is that Kyrano–'

'Stop calling him that,' I snapped. 'Whoever he was before, that thing is a servitor now.'

'Of course, yes,' said Garrett. 'You're right, of course. I'll have another room prepared for you immediately. I shall see to it personally.'

'What are you going to do about the servitor?'

'There's a man in town,' said Garrett. 'Not a tech-priest as such, but he has a knack with cybernetics. Used to work in the vehicle pool as part of the enginseer cohorts. Maintains most of the old cargo-eights around here. I'll have him take a look at Kyr– the servitor today, do a fresh memory-cache scrub.'

'Fine, but do it today or I am leaving.'

'Absolutely. No question,' said Garrett. 'And please, take today to rest and recover. Whatever it was that happened in the night must have been traumatic.'

I bit back an angry retort to *whatever it was*. While Garrett Grayloc was in the mood for concessions, I had one last thing to ask him.

'Do the initials *M.R.* mean anything to you?'

He thought for a moment before answering.

'It could be Montague Rhodes, why?'

Unwilling to yet disclose the existence of the monogrammed journal I had studied last night, I decided obfuscation was the best course of action.

'I found his initials in a number of the colonel's books,' I said. 'Who is he?'

'I believe he was the custodian of my mother's library,' said Garrett.

'*Was?*'

'Yes. He retired soon after my mother's death. I heard the poor fellow was quite distraught at her loss. He and his wife still live down in the town, I believe.'

I nodded, now knowing how I would spend the rest of this day.

I left Grayloc Manor as soon as I could and walked back down into Vansen Falls. Garrett claimed to have no knowledge as to where exactly Montague Rhodes lived, but I had a good idea of where to start.

Making my way to Gant's Confectionary and Recaff Emporium, I purchased another sugared pastry that felt deliciously comforting and engaged in awkward small talk until I found a way to enquire after Colonel Grayloc's previous librarian.

'A terrible business,' he said, leading me to believe that this must be a favourite phrase around Vansen Falls. 'Poor fellow. Was never the same after the colonel died, Emperor rest her soul.'

'What happened to him?'

'Books were his life, you see, Mistress Sullo,' said Gant. 'He'd curated her books for decades, knew that collection inside out. When Master Garrett came back and announced he was going to sell them off, well, it quite broke the fellow's mind.'

'As you say, a terrible business,' I said, with enough

of an upwards inflection that Gant might feel the urge
to continue.

'Indeed it was,' agreed Gant. 'Poor fellow lost his mind.
Too aghast at all the colonel's books being scattered
to the wind, I suppose. Can't remember the last time
I saw him. Only ever see his wife, Odette. And even
then, rarely.'

I nodded and said, 'The thing is, Master Gant, I've
encountered a rather knotty issue in my cataloguing,
and it would be most helpful were I able to consult
with Master Rhodes. Do you happen to know where I
might be able to call upon him?'

Gant was indeed able to furnish me with an address,
and after only a mild diversion in the twisting streets
of Vansen Falls, I found myself before a sturdy door of
pale wood set in a low, clay-tiled cottage overlooking
the ocean on the northern curve of the crater. Smoke
issued from a leaning chimney, and I could not help but
be slightly unsettled to see that each of the windows
was shuttered, and that the shutters had been nailed
into their frames.

My first knocks went unanswered, but I persisted,
suspecting that the cottage's inhabitants would not be
the sort of people to wander far from their place of
sanctuary.

Eventually the door was opened by an elderly woman
who wore the cares of the world upon her face. She
eyed me suspiciously, her appraisal visibly swift and
brutal.

'What do you want?' she said.

'I'm sorry to disturb you, but are you Odette?' I asked.

She nodded, but volunteered no further information.

'My name is Teresina Sullo, and I would very much like to speak to your husband.'

Odette's expression, already wary, hardened to outright hostility and she began to shut the door in my face. I stepped in close to prevent its closing.

'Please,' I said. 'I need his help.'

'He can't help anyone,' said Odette. 'Not any more.'

I had one last gamble before the door was closed for good.

'It's about Valgaast,' I said.

The interior of the cottage was dark, which was only to be expected given that its heavy shutters were kept permanently sealed. I felt as though the light that entered with the opening of the door was an unwilling guest, one that gratefully fled with its closing.

Odette led me to a sealed room towards the back of the cottage and hesitated before it.

'You won't get anything from him,' she promised. 'No one does.'

'I need to speak with him,' I insisted.

'You can speak, but he won't be answering.'

I couldn't help but feel she was offering me a last chance to withdraw. Even now I wonder how things might have transpired had I done so.

'Please,' I said.

She sighed, lifting a key from a pocket at her waist and unlocking the door.

The room beyond was musty and stifling, and the

stench filled me with the urge to flee, for I sensed nothing but reeking madness within and a life sustained at a cost not worth paying.

I looked back at Odette. She bore the expression of a woman trying to quell something entirely intolerable. Reluctantly, I stepped inside and felt my gorge rise at the thickness of the air, as much a prisoner within as the old man slumped in a chair before an empty hearth.

No daylight reached this room, and only a pair of tallow candles set upon the mantle provided any illumination. Montague Rhodes sat with his back to me, staring into the cold fireplace as if hoping flames might spring forth to consume him and the cottage both. From the doorway, I could only see the top of his hairless pate, wrinkled and spotted with age.

'Master Rhodes?'

His head tilted a fraction at the sound of his name, but he did not turn nor rise from his chair. I had known men and women who had, through age or injury, been forced to abandon their vocations and who had swiftly sunk into depression or listlessness. But, according to Garrett, Montague Rhodes had only recently left the colonel's employ.

Surely he could not have sunk so low so soon?

Slowly I approached his chair.

A low stool was set in front of the old man's chair. I circled it and sat down before him.

He lifted his head and I gasped at the horrid ruin of his face. I had hoped to converse with him, archivist to archivist, but I now saw that would be impossible.

Montague's eyes had been destroyed, gouged out of his

skull. The flesh around his sockets was raw and muti-
lated with deep-ploughed furrows, tearing wounds cut
by ragged glass and sealed with sutures. My hand flew
to my mouth, horrified at the scale and severity of his
wounds; wounds I knew with an absolute certainty I
cannot now explain were self-inflicted.

His thin body was swathed in woollen blankets, and
I saw his protruding hands were restrained by thick
leather straps. My gorge rose as I saw the fingers of
his left hand were gone, only ragged stumps remaining
beneath a filthy bandage. The image of him hacking
them away with the same bloodied glass that had taken
his eyes flashed into my mind. His right hand still possessed its digits but they were broken and useless, as
though he had punched them against steel until the
bones within had been reduced to powder.

'Master Rhodes?' I said again.

He did not answer, but swung his head towards me,
like a burrowing creature suddenly aware of nearby
predators. His cracked and dry lips parted and he drew
breath. A soft sound began in his throat, and I leaned
closer to hear what he had to say.

His jaw fell open and I recoiled as I saw the ragged
wet nub of lacerated meat that was all that remained of
his tongue. This was no surgical incision, but the result
of frenzied slicing with something jagged and not quite
sharp enough to cut cleanly. The inside of Montague's
mouth was filled with poorly healed stab wounds and
broken teeth.

'Throne!' I cried, almost falling from the stool.

I turned towards Odette.

'Emperor's Mercy, what happened to him?'

'That manor at the top of the promontory happened to him,' she said, circling her stricken husband and stroking his head. 'The books he read. The colonel's very own words. The things she saw, things she did. *The things she brought back...*'

'I don't understand.'

'Colonel Grayloc, they say she was a hero, yes?'

'She is,' I said. 'She was able to fight her way back to the Imperium after the Dawn of Dark Suns when all others fell.'

'So many died,' said Odette. 'Did you never wonder *how* she made it back?'

'By all accounts, Elena Grayloc was an exemplary leader, and her soldiers were some of the very best.'

'The 83rd were good soldiers, some of the very best,' agreed Odette. 'But no one is *that* good. They all should have died. No one could have lived through that, but *she* did. She and those she trusted to come with her, *no matter what*. Imagine what that cost her, how much of her humanity she would've had to surrender along the way.'

'How do you know all this?' I asked.

Odette knelt beside her husband.

His head turned this way and that, as if straining to hear a far-distant song. I wondered how much he could understand of what we were saying.

Odette gently placed a hand on his arm and said, 'My Montague, he found her memoirs.'

My heart leapt with excitement I did my best to conceal.

'He found the colonel's monograph?'

'For all the good it did him.'

'What do you mean?'

Odette rose from her knees and said, 'I've heard about you, Mistress Sullo. You're going through the colonel's books, yes?'

'Yes. Garrett Grayloc intends to sell them to cover his mother's debts.'

Odette moved around the back of her husband's chair and rested her hand on his shoulder.

'You should leave this place,' she said to me. 'Now, while you still can. I ought to have warned you earlier, but I couldn't leave my Montague. The books... the things he read... they drove him mad, you see. The horror of learning what happened out there in the Ocyllaria subsector, it broke his mind. The day it was finally too much... he came home, the words just spilling out of him in a flood, like he couldn't stop it. He was saying awful things, vile things...'

'What things?'

'Things I won't repeat,' said Odette, and I saw a memory of the most hideous slurs imaginable pass over her face. 'He knew he was saying them, he was weeping the whole time, but it was like he couldn't stop saying them. He kept trying to stop, but the words inside kept boiling out of him.'

I could see revisiting these memories was traumatic for Odette, but I needed to know what had happened, what Montague had found.

'Did he ever mention Val–'

Odette's hand snapped out and clamped over my

mouth. Her skin tasted of fish and the stale sweat of a locked room.

She glanced down at Montague and shook her head slowly. 'Don't say it.'

I nodded as she lifted her hand away and continued.

'So he's ranting and raving like a madman, and *that* word you were about to say comes out of his mouth. No sooner does it pass his lips than he gets up and smashes his fist into the mirror. Breaks it to pieces and picks up a long shard like a carving knife. Takes it to his tongue first, then his eyes. All the time I'm screaming and trying to stop him, but he's stronger than he looks and he throws me off. No sooner are his eyes and tongue gone than he's looking for parchment and quill, like what was in him was trying to find a way out, *any way out*. He starts scratching random numbers on a page he'd torn from his old journal. As soon as he's done, he takes the same glass that cut out his eyes and tongue and hacks his fingers away back to the palm. When he realised he couldn't do the same to the hand he had left, he just punched the wall until it was nothing but bloody flesh and bone fragments.'

All through Odette's tale, I sat incredulous, transfixed by the horror Montague Rhodes had wrought upon his own flesh.

'What could have been so terrible that it would warrant such horrifying self-mutilation?'

'I don't know,' said Odette. 'I don't *want* to know. And neither should you.'

'Do you think something similar happened to the colonel?'

Odette's eyes narrowed. 'What do you mean?'

'I heard she fell from the cliffs of the manor during the storm,' I said. 'Perhaps her death wasn't an accident? Perhaps she too was afflicted by these... *visions*, and that drove her to hurl herself from the cliff?'

Odette gave me a look of the kind I had not seen since my days in the scholam when the drill abbots were displeased with me.

'You're half right,' allowed Odette.

'What does *that* mean?'

'It means the colonel's death wasn't an accident, but it wasn't a suicide either.'

'So what was it?'

'Boatman that found her said her head was mostly gone, split wide open, and empty like a cracked egg.'

'Those cliffs are high. The impact of landing could easily explain such a wound.'

'That they are, but the boatman is ex-Guard,' said Odette. 'He saw more than one commissar perform a summary execution.'

Odette saw my look of confusion and said, 'Point is, he knows what a gunshot to the back of the head looks like.'

I did not linger much longer in that awful cottage, and the memory of Montague Rhodes still sends a surge of revulsion through me, though now I have a better understanding of what motivated him to take the mirror-glass to his face.

As I stood in the doorway of the cottage, Odette pressed a folded sheet of paper into my palm and said,

'Take it. I don't want it in here a moment longer. Maybe it'll help you, or maybe you should just burn it.'

She retreated and closed the door before I could ask any more.

I felt desperately sorry for Odette and her husband, but I stepped quickly away from their cottage, wanting to put as much distance between myself and the despair that lay within like a sickness. I could feel the dank texture of trapped air leaving my lungs with every step I took and each breath of sea air.

I was not yet ready to return to Grayloc Manor, so made my way to Gant's emporium. I intended to purchase a hot mug of caffeine, hoping to impart some warmth to my limbs and to drive away the ice that had settled in my bones. I needed time to process all I had learned from Odette's tale. How much of it could be true, and what did it mean?

I took a seat in a secluded booth at the rear and nursed my drink, now understanding how little I really knew, and how much more there was to Colonel Grayloc's life.

Could the colonel have been murdered?

If so, by whom, and why?

What terrors were concealed within the monograph that had driven Montague Rhodes to inflict such terrible injuries upon himself? What danger was I in just being here? And, most important of all, could I endure what he had not?

Those were questions I could not answer with my limited knowledge. I sipped my drink and reached into the pocket of my robes to lift out the journal and see if any new insights might reveal themselves. I thumbed through its pages until I came to the ragged edges at the gutter where two of its pages had been ripped out.

Unfolding the paper Odette had handed me, I laid it flat next to the torn edges.

Its edges perfectly matched up, unequivocally establishing its provenance.

The paper had been crumped since being torn out, and dried bloodstains were smeared across it. I could imagine Odette, having balled up the page in grief, standing before the hearth and debating whether or not to throw it in the fire. I wondered why she had not, as I wondered why she had thought to pass it on to me.

The page was filled with a repeating series of six numbers.

The handwriting was familiar to me, the frantic etchings of a damaged psyche. Like the later writings in the journal it was hard to read, but given the circumstance in which these numbers had been set down, it was a miracle any of this was legible at all. What could be so important about these numbers that the last remaining scraps of sanity the old man possessed had driven him to record them after stabbing a glass dagger into both his eyeballs?

I stared at them for hours, willing them to reveal their significance. Running a finger over the paper, I felt the rough texture of its pressed fibres, the raised ridge-lines of dried ink.

Was there a sequence or order to these numbers?

Was there a sequ–

And then I knew.

* * *

After speaking with Odette and seeing the ruin of her husband, I had little desire to return to Grayloc Manor, but the promise of what I might discover were my suspicions correct was too great to resist. The sun was well past its zenith, and I felt no warmth from it as a stiff gale blew in from the ocean.

The curve of the crater spun ocean spume into vortices of mist and seawater, such that I felt as though I was walking uphill through a veil of tears. Looking out to sea, it was clear the storm that had long threatened to break overhead now seemed on the verge of unleashing its fury. Though it was only mid-afternoon, the sky was the textured grey of napped flint, and the dark clouds over the ocean were racing to the coast at a rate of knots.

I glanced back at the temple on the opposite headland, its lonely spire stark against the clouds. Now that I knew the truth of its condition, it was impossible not to feel the absence of the Emperor's presence in Vansen Falls.

'The Emperor protects,' I whispered as I approached the manor, but the memory of the destroyed temple made my words ring hollow. I saw no lights within the manor, all its windows as black as the void of space.

Taking care to make as little noise as possible, I entered the manor like a thief, not wishing to attract any attention. I hoped to test my theory undisturbed, and the approaching storm abetted me in this as a peal of thunder rumbled overhead.

The house felt deserted, which perfectly suited my purpose as I climbed the stairs towards the library. A sudden burst of rain beat a tattoo against the windows. Howling winds whistled around the eaves.

Darkness held sway within the house. No lights were lit, but I knew my way around enough not to need more than the last of the day's light spilling in through the rain-smeared windows. Swiftly, I made my way to the red doors of the colonel's library. I paused to listen at the door, but could hear nothing more than the creak of settling timbers and rattling roof tiles. Satisfied the library was empty, I entered and closed the door behind me.

Thunder rolled again, louder this time.

A flash of lightning illuminated the colonel's formal portrait and the weapons beneath it.

Taking a moment to quell my rising anticipation, I let out a shuddering breath and unfolded the paper Odette had given me.

1, 6, 15, 28, 45, 61.

My time in the library had given me a deep familiarity with its layout, and I made my way to the shelf inset with the numbered ceramic disc labelled with a 1.

I laid my fingertip against it and felt the tiniest sensation of potential movement. Taking a deep breath, I pressed the disc, and my heart leapt as I was rewarded with a soft click, like a tumbler rolling in the barrel of a lock. Moving from shelf to shelf, I located each number in turn and pressed. Each time, it clicked with the sound of a turning key.

Despite everything I had learned and my growing sense of standing at the edge of something I could barely comprehend, I could scarce contain a giddy sense of excitement as I stood before the last shelf.

I pressed the disc marked 61 and waited.

For long seconds, nothing happened. All I could hear was the rising winds encircling Grayloc Manor, but then I heard the ratcheting clockwork sounds of an elaborate mechanism coming into some preordained configuration.

I turned to see a portion of the floor sliding back to reveal a set of stone steps leading down into darkness. A flash of lightning illuminated a short stairwell. The musky bouquet of Fireblooms wafted up from below, and I had the impression of a much larger space beneath.

I had found what I was looking for, yet still I hesitated.

My mouth was dry. Suddenly I wasn't sure I *wanted* to know what lay below.

Was this where Colonel Grayloc kept her monograph?

Surely so secret a room was too great a precaution for any book, even one so singular?

What else might the colonel keep hidden below? What was it Odette had said?

The things she brought back...

But I had come too far to turn away now, so I descended into the darkness with hesitant steps, each one feeling like it might be my last.

Dust lay thick on the stone floor of the room below, and the musty air of something spoiled was hard to miss, even over the potency of the Firebloom petals that lay scattered like confetti. My nose wrinkled at the smell – like soured fruit or an overpowering perfume.

The room beneath the library was akin to a study, lit by an oil-fuelled storm lantern that threw dancing shadows upon walls lined with shelves. Most of these were empty, but those that were not held disturbing statuettes carved from a strange greenish soapstone whose grotesque and monstrous anatomies were thankfully obscured by the gloom. A few books stood in splendid isolation, as though some past librarian – Montague perhaps? – had come upon them and not dared remove these particular volumes of forgotten lore.

The remains of packing crates and scraps of wax paper lay discarded in a corner, telling me that whatever books and artefacts had once lined these shelves had long gone.

But where were they now?

My skin crawled just to look upon the books that remained, for the texture of their bindings was, even in this low light, impossible to mistake for anything other than skin.

Why would a colonel of the Astra Militarum possess such things…?

I could not bring myself to touch any of these books and thus learn their titles. Just being near them made me feel unclean and violated in the most profound way.

But worse than the hideous books, the fundamental *wrongness* of this space was impossible to ignore.

I knew from my time at Grayloc Manor that the dining room lay directly beneath the library. This space should not be able to exist. So blatant a violation of the natural physical laws set my teeth on edge and the contents of my stomach churning.

I could not bear to be here, but nor could I leave.

My body was at war with competing sensations of revulsion and the desire to know more.

My heart beat fast in my chest as I walked an ever-decreasing circle around the single table and chair in the centre of this impossible space. The lantern cast a fitful illumination over two books laid upon the table as though awaiting a reader to unlock their secrets. I felt unhealthily drawn to these books, as though an invisible cord linked me to them and was being wound tighter with every step I took.

No, these books weren't waiting for just any reader, they were waiting for me.

Denying the inevitable seemed pointless at this stage, so I pulled the chair back and sat down, feeling like my entire life and career had led me to this time and place.

The first book was thinner, and appeared to be a nondescript accounting ledger, while the second bore a cover stamped with the aquila and skull symbol of the Astra Militarum. While researching the campaigns of Lord Militant General Hexior Padira III during my time at the Cardophian Repository, my team and I had studied countless commanders' records kept in just such books.

Though it wasn't the same book as painted in the colonel's portrait, it bore the same circular symbol pierced by an arrow that book had possessed. I felt certain that this was the book that Garrett Grayloc and I had long sought.

Reluctant to touch this item, I instead lifted the ledger and scanned its contents.

The pages were arranged in columns and were filled with titles, dates, amounts of money and locations. It took the recognition of unwelcomely familiar titles I had seen in Montague Rhodes' journal for me to realise what I held. I looked up at the empty shelves as a rancid knot of horror made a clenched fist in my belly.

This was a record of the various locations to which the books in this study had been despatched. Some had been sent off-world to fellow connoisseurs of the perverse, others to hive nobility across Yervaunt. But a great many had been sent to the Cardophian Repository.

The texts in the library above were occasionally risqué, sometimes ill-advised to own, or borderline illegal, but every title I could bear to read in the ledger was utterly proscribed, a heretical book that would see its owner immediately executed for even knowing about, let alone possessing.

The things she brought back…

Colonel Grayloc had spread a host of blasphemous books throughout the subsector like a virus, and altogether too many were housed in *my* repository. Who knew what damage they were doing or how many innocents had become tainted by the heresy they contained?

I was hyperventilating at the scale of Colonel Grayloc's treachery, and I put the ledger back on the table as my eyes drifted to the larger book. This had to be the monograph Garrett Grayloc had spoken of, and though I absolutely did *not* want to look at what lay within, I knew that I must.

I had to have an explanation. I had to know *why* Colonel Grayloc had chosen to collect these hideous books and wilfully spread their blasphemous knowledge.

She was a hero of the Imperium, and her betrayal was a knife in my heart.

Tears streamed down my face as I opened the colonel's monograph and began to read.

I have studied the writings of many great men and women, the words of saints and traitors alike. Throughout my life, the written word has made me laugh, made me weep, brought me joy and pierced me with sorrow.

In all its forms it has brought me knowledge, wonder and escape.

The monograph of Elena Grayloc was the first book I wished I could unread.

It began innocuously enough, but soon descended into madness.

I cannot bring myself to set down every hideous detail of what was recorded in that damned book, a mercy for which you should be thankful. I suspected there were many journals before this, ones that dealt with the logistics of commanding a sector-wide campaign, but I never found them. By the time the words in the monograph had been written, however, the very worst canker had taken root in Elena Grayloc's soul.

Her descent into treachery began sometime after the liberation of Heliogabalus, a hive world where a debased pleasure cult had taken root in the noble family of an Imperial commander named Aphra Verlaine. The corruption had swiftly spread to his ancestral allies, ultimately resulting in a devastating civil war that spilled over into neighbouring systems.

Elena Grayloc had led her Tempestus Scions in a decapitating strike against Verlaine's palace, fighting their way to his throne room through hordes of shrieking cultists whose bodies had been transformed by grotesque sur-geries and mutagenic drugs. Elaborate descriptions and detailed anatomical drawings of the foe were recorded in the monograph, abominations and things of such hor-ror that it seemed impossible they could live beyond a single breath.

With the death of Aphra Verlaine, the Archenemy forces fell into disarray, the tide of the war turned, and Heliogabalus was liberated.

I cannot say for sure how her fall to darkness began; an artefact taken from the palace that carried with it some taint, a wound that festered and corrupted her from within. Or mayhap some psychic spoor of Ver-laine's was laid within her skull that day. However it came to pass, when Elena Grayloc left Heliogabalus, it was as a servant of darkness.

Perhaps learning from what had befallen Aphra Ver-laine, the corruption began to spread slowly through the regiment with a subtle insidiousness. A number of new martial customs and practices were established in every company, practices that allowed the evil of Chaos to corrupt every Guardsman within the regiment: tainted litanies of battle, blasphemous iconography, and a broadening of the rules of engagement that encouraged debauched conduct in the aftermath of battle.

With every campaign, the behaviour of the 83rd grew ever more hideous, with Colonel Grayloc overseeing scenes of mass murder, torture and depravity I could scarcely bear to read. Their victims were men and women, mothers, children and babes in arms. All were mere sport for the soldiers and officers of the regiment, their bodies simply canvasses upon which they wrought the most monstrous of evils.

Colonel Grayloc saw to it that her regiment was deployed on the front lines of the most hellish warzones, theatres of conflict where the terror of their debasements and horror of their actions could more easily be concealed. Each victory against Archenemy forces saw yet more artefacts and tomes concealed from the quarantine teams of the ordos and despatched in secret to Grayloc Manor.

Perhaps to the very study in which I now sat.

My skin crawled at the thought of sitting in a room where so many cursed tomes and blasphemous artefacts had once been stored. What evil had seeped from their pages and into the very air? Was that what the Fireblooms were to conceal, the rank stench of perfidy?

I looked up from the flickering light cast by the storm-lantern, fear making me see monsters in the shadows on the walls and hear the muttering of the damned in the rumbles of thunder coming from the library above.

I had no wish to return to the colonel's monograph, but I felt compelled to read more.

On and on it went, revelling in heinous excesses. A carnivale of grotesqueries followed in the regiment's wake until finally, at the height of the terrible wars in the Ocyllaria subsector, the rumours surrounding the truth of Colonel Grayloc's regiment came to a head.

With mounting horror, I read of the colonel's frustrations as the net closed in on her corrupted regiment. Her every effort, combined with the fury of war and the capriciousness of the warp, had conspired to conceal their depravities for longer than ought to have been possible, but eventually the truth of their utter corruption could not be denied.

Imperial agents of the Holy Ordos, combined with elements of the Adepta Sororitas, at last moved against Colonel Grayloc, but it was already too late.

Sensing her enemies closing in, Elena Grayloc committed the ultimate betrayal of her species. Thankfully, I could not fully understand the nature of what she did, nor how she did it, but it seems clear she used the tainted artefacts in her possession to call for aid from the dark prince she now called master. Her words described this moment of apotheosis thusly:

'...a wondrous veil fell across the world, a shroud of Night, a tide of darkness to devour the slaves of the rotting corpse god. It rolled ever on, a black tide that spilled like tainted seed to corrupt the land with its glorious boon. And when it had supped all the life and vigour of this world, it reached up into the heavens to quench its endless thirst, and, one by one, snuffed out the stars as easily as I might douse a candle flame.'

I could barely draw breath by this point. Tears streamed down my face as the full extent of what Elena Grayloc had done became clear.

She had caused the Dawn of Dark Suns and killed everyone who knew of her sins.

The deaths of millions of men and women of the Astra Militarum lay upon her soul. Their blood was a red ocean upon her hands.

And her superiors had unwittingly rewarded her for it!

The sickness in my gut was almost too much to bear.

My heart pounded within my chest. Blood thundered in my ears.

Every time I thought I could not bear to read more, my eyes were irresistibly drawn back to the silken pages.

I took a deep, calming breath that helped not at all. I needed to know more.

After her monstrous crime, Colonel Grayloc returned to Yervaunt and, for a time it seemed, sought to curb her unholy appetites. I imagine they were harder to conceal without a war to cover the excesses of blood and depravity. But the blight on her soul would not be so easily restrained, and Grayloc Manor became a locus for those of like desires. Gatherings of the wicked and the damned became common. Dubbed *Maraviglia*, these were days-long debauches of sense-heightening drugs, unnatural couplings of orgiastic intensity, and ritual-ised murder that sent such jolts of revulsion through my mind that I feared for my very sanity.

I read accounts of men and women variously described as sensationalists, gourmands, profligates, epicures and libertines, who journeyed from afar and even from off-world to partake in the colonel's wild debauches. The descriptions of seething flesh, blood, bodily fluids and vile acts made me sick to picture them.

These guests came to the hidden jetty at the foot of the cliffs or arrived under cover of night at her cliffside landing platform. The descriptions of these *Maraviglia* defied belief, and the *activities* described were so outrageous and so unimaginable that I now understood the calamitous nature of the colonel's debts.

With trembling fingers, I closed the colonel's monograph.

I covered my face with my hands, weeping and shaking with the horror of what I had learned. My eyes were tightly shut, but upon the inner surfaces of my eyelids I saw only screaming faces twisted in lust, in anguish and in agony.

Each arrhythmic crash in my chest made me fear for my life. The rush of blood through my head felt like hammer blows upon my skull.

Then I understood that the pounding noise was not just in my head.

Heavy footfalls were descending the steps from the library.

I took my hands from my face, too terrified to move.

A brutish outline filled the doorway, a glowing storm-lantern held aloft before him.

Kyrano.

I rose from the chair on shaking legs as the servitor strode towards me with relentless purpose. He had already tried to murder me once before, and I knew I was powerless to stop him from succeeding this time.

'Please,' I begged the cybernetic as he approached.

I screamed as loud as I could, filling the small space with my anger and terror. It did no good, and Kyrano cared nothing for any noise I made. For all I knew the servitor and I were the only two souls left alive in Grayloc Manor.

Where was Garrett Grayloc? Had the servitor already murdered him in his sleep?

Was this *thing* still enacting Elena Grayloc's deviant orders beyond her death?

The servitor circled the table, and I could already imagine how his hands would feel around my neck as they crushed my throat. He would kill me with no remorse, no passion, and no care for the evil of what he was doing.

My legs spasmed with frantic tremors, the muscles twitching as my anger at this fate railed against the paralysis of terror. I pushed back from the table, thankful for its scale, as I circled in the opposite direction to the approaching servitor.

I could not hope to fight him, but perhaps I could delay him or, at the very least, hurt him.

Leaning over the table, I snatched up the storm lantern. Kyrano reached out to grab me, his fingers closing on my sleeve. Thankfully, his fingers had no real purchase, and his grip slid free. For a moment, it seemed I saw frustration in his one remaining eye, a hooded, flinty thing that had peered into the heart of true evil.

Glancing towards the stairs leading back to the library, I tried to imagine how quickly I could cover the distance. Could I outrun Kyrano?

He was not fast, but he was utterly relentless.

I judged my chances poor, but what other choice was there?

Feinting one way, I bolted for the stairs. Faster than I would have believed possible, the murderous servitor came after me. I heard the thud of his booted feet behind me and reacted with an act of instinctive self-preservation.

I swung the storm lantern like a club and managed to smash it against the side of his metalled skull. Burning oil flared in a sheet of bright orange fire. It filled the hidden study with light, and engulfed the servitor's upper body in flame.

Pools of burning oil landed on the table and hungrily spread to the two books. I hurled the smashed remains of the lantern to the floor and ran for the stairs, taking them two at a time. I did not look back, and heard the servitor thrashing around the study.

I had not thought servitors capable of feeling pain, but was in that moment glad it seemed not to be the case here. I hoped the flames would consume Kyrano and whatever was left upon the shelves.

Smoke followed me up the stairs, and I took a shuddering breath as I emerged into the library. Rain hammered on the skylights and a forking bolt of lightning split the sky. I drew in sucking breaths of air, wondering if I could somehow seal off the study and trap the murderous servitor below.

A flare of light behind me told me I had no time.

Kyrano was climbing the stairs after me. The flames had burned away much of his suit, revealing the scorched skin of his torso. Beaten metal gleamed through pallid skin criss-crossed with crude surgical scars that looked as though they had been inflicted as much to hurt as to heal.

I turned and ran for the library doors, pausing as I saw the stern face of Colonel Grayloc staring down at me from the frame of her portrait. Even then, in full knowledge of her monstrous deeds and the millions of lives she sacrificed, I could see no hint of that evil lurking in her eyes. She appeared to be every inch the Imperial hero she was believed to be. That such depravity and such a black and soulless heart could hide in plain sight behind a mask of civility and a veneer of civilisation was the true horror.

Evil walked amongst us and we knew it not.

Thudding footsteps galvanised me into action, and I ran to the portrait to seize the weapons hung beneath it. I have no love of firearms, but Teodoro and I both held to the view that every Imperial citizen ought to at least maintain a basic competence with weaponry.

The weapons were old, and neither had likely been fired in years.

I could see the plasma pistol had no powercell in place, so snatched the lasrifle down from its mount, quickly hauling back on the charging lever by the trigger guard. Even a Whiteshield knows to strip an unknown weapon down before risking pulling the trigger, but that was a luxury I could not afford.

The lasrifle hummed as power flowed into its firing mechanism, but any hopes of using the weapon died as the powercell registered as empty. I wanted to weep with frustration.

I dropped the lasrifle and took up Colonel Grayloc's power sabre. I thumbed the activation rune at the pommel. Even if its charge was depleted, I could at least swing it and hope its edge was sharp.

Footsteps sounded, and I gagged at the thought of the servitor's rotten-meat body touching me. A deafening rumble of thunder crashed overhead. I thought I heard my name. The blade sparked to life. I screamed as I spun around and swung it with all my strength.

The energised edge struck flesh, carving through meat

and bone, muscle and organs. Blood sprayed from the wound, a catastrophic amount jetting from ruptured flesh. It sprayed my face, blinding me. I ripped the blade loose and lifted it high, ready to strike again.

I blinked away the blood in my eyes.

I had not killed Kyrano.

I had killed Garrett Grayloc.

His body lay on the floor of the library in a vast lake of blood, split from collarbone to pelvis. I backed away in horror at what I had done. His head turned to me, incomprehension flickering in his eyes as the last vestiges of life left him.

'No... no... no...' I cried, as though forceful enough a denial might undo this murder.

I saw him die in front of me, and looked up as I saw Kyrano approach. Smoke and flames lit the library behind him, and he no longer had his storm lantern. I saw him register the presence of Garrett Grayloc's body, but could not tell what reaction – if any – his master's death had upon him.

Still holding the colonel's sword, I ran for the library doors, barrelling through them, breathless and horrified at what I had done. My entire body was shaking with fear and revulsion. What had I done? I had killed an innocent man! I bent double and expelled the contents of my stomach on the floor.

I wanted to sink to my knees and curl up into a ball. I wanted this tide of horrible things to stop, to leave me alone. My mind could not cope with so many nightmarish revelations, with such bloodshed and murder.

Looking back into the library, I saw Kyrano bend to

lift the lasrifle from the floor where I had thrown it. He expertly swapped out the empty powercell for a fresh one and rose smoothly as he snapped back the charging lever to render it lethal.

Even armed with the power sabre I could not fight a deadly killer armed with a rifle.

'No,' I said, but this time the word was not said in reaction to an accidental murder, rather it was a declaration that I would not end my days squatting and afraid.

Pushing myself upright, I ran for the staircase that led down to the vestibule.

I emerged from Grayloc Manor into a thunderstorm of epic proportions. Bruised clouds of lightning-shot darkness pressed down on the landscape, and a deluge set to drown the world fell from the sky in howling torrents. The power sabre spat and hissed as I half ran, half stumbled around the corner of the building.

Looking out to sea, the storm was even more impressive.

Purple and blue columns of lightning battled on the horizon and the normally calm bay within the crater raged against the coastline. I saw ships smashed to tinder at their moorings, and pummelling waves broke against structures hundreds of metres from the shoreline.

Across the headland, the temple was in flames, and not even the downpour could quench the conflagration. And was it my imagination or did I see the figure of a man in priestly vestments within, vainly attempting to fight the blaze?

I could think of no more apt a metaphor of my time in Vansen Falls.

I turned the corner, heading for the cliffside hangar where the Kiehlen 580 groundcar was housed. If I could just get the car, I could escape this nightmare. I passed the winding path leading to the follies, and stopped at the entrance to the maze as I saw my path to the hangar was blocked.

Kyrano stood illuminated in the glow of the burning manor. Flames leapt from its gable windows and billowed high from the shattered skylights in the library.

I had stupidly assumed the servitor would blindly follow me, but of course he would take the more direct route. He must have anticipated I would run to the hangar and had chosen a route to intercept my flight.

His augmetic eye blinked red and he marched towards me, seemingly untroubled by the horrific wounds wrought upon his body. The rain slicked his ruined flesh, and he held the colonel's rife across his chest. My strike with the storm lantern had wounded him terribly, the burning fuel devouring his dead skin and leaving him all but crippled.

But even crippled he would easily kill me.

His pace was unrelenting. Not fast, but fast enough to catch me no matter where I ran.

Heading for the follies seemed foolish, so I turned and entered the maze. My only hope was that Kyrano did not know its paths. Or even if he did, that I could navigate them faster and emerge while he was still within.

Perhaps then I could reach the groundcar and escape.

I plunged into its tangled depths.

The rain beat down as I pushed deep into the maze, washing my face of tears. My feet slipped on the muddy paths, and several times I fell as I lost my footing. Thunder crashed, but even over its echoing rumbles, I could still hear Kyrano following me.

I blundered through the maze, scratching my face bloody on grasping thorns and deactivating the sabre's blade. I had no idea how much power was left to it, and saw no need to drain what little remained until I needed it.

I struggled to focus as I ran, remembering the times I had navigated the maze and committed its paths to memory. I prayed to the Emperor I was remembering things correctly, and that Kyrano had not seen fit to walk within or learn its many twists and turns.

It was perhaps a vain and desperate hope, but it was the only hope I had.

I pushed onwards, turning and pressing ever deeper into the maze, not knowing if any turn would bring me face to face with the servitor. I gripped the sabre tight, ready to swing it again if I saw him. My hands were shaking, and I tried to keep the memory of Garrett Grayloc's ruptured body from my mind. I knew that if I let thoughts of what I had done consume me, then I would be overwhelmed and lost.

At last I emerged into the centre of the maze, and let out a strangled cry of relief.

The strangely androgynous statue of pinkish coral gleamed in the rain, its surfaces slick and dripping with water. I stumbled forwards and all but collapsed onto the marble bench encircling it, gasping for breath.

I needed to move. I needed to get back out to reach the groundcar.

But I had nothing left to draw upon. My reserves of strength and resilience were spent.

The driving rain and crashing waves were oddly muted through the crooked hedgerows of the maze, but I could hear a curious sound, the source of which I could not at first identify.

A splitting sound, like hairline cracks spreading through a pane of glass.

The tenor of the sound changed, becoming the wet sucking noise of something being pulled from the cloying grasp of a swamp. The rain was beating down harder now, and another flash of lightning bathed the sky in violet light.

My memory flew back to the long causeway traversing the hideous marshland that so disquieted me on my journey to Grayloc Manor. My mind flooded with images of dead and misbegotten things festering unseen in the dark.

I turned slowly as I felt a growing sensation of warmth behind me.

Now I understood the source of the sound, and the fraying weave of my sanity begin to unravel yet further.

The statue at the centre of the maze was *moving*.

It rippled with a grotesque internal movement, its once rigid structure now pliant as though the torrential rain had softened it. No longer did it appear to be made of ridged and nubbed coral, but of pinkish folds of layered flesh that were unfolding like a night-blooming flower. It stretched and swelled, as if something confined within its moist innards was struggling to push itself free.

Like a newborn pushing against the membrane of an egg sac...

Even as I watched, the stretched *skin* of the statue tore in a jagged, vertical line. Blood and fluid spilled from the rent, and the stench of burnt sugar drove me to my feet as the mass of the statue peeled away like meat no longer supported by a skeleton.

Embedded within the folds of flesh were splintered bone shards, scores of gleaming teeth and discarded networks of veins and half-digested organs.

And in the centre of this mass was a bent and crooked figure.

Its wrinkled and ancient skin was wet and slathered with a clear, amniotic slime, like the princeps of a battle Titan removed from its command tank. The awful thing faced away from me, and I saw a blasted hole in the back of its head like a gunshot wound. Threads of light and gossamer-thin flesh held the skull together, and but for them, the creature's cranium would have collapsed to ruin long ago.

Long silver hair clung to its hunched and twisted back, and beneath the translucent skin, I saw a spine that had been shattered by some ferocious impact.

Like falling from a cliff...

The thing turned to face me, and its awful, ravaged appearance was horribly familiar.

The patrician features, the eyes of rich gold-green...

Elena Grayloc.

I fell into the maelstrom of her eyes.

She was the most beautiful human being I had ever seen.

Young and filled with the vitality only those who have never known loss can possess. This was Elena Grayloc before her long years in the Astra Militarum, an idealised version of the person she believed herself to be.

Her eyes met mine, and the sound of the storm was instantly replaced by the soft sound of gentle waves lapping on a beach. Sunlight bathed me, and I trembled at the feeling of a silken touch winding its way around the back of my neck.

'Auburn suits you,' she said in a whispered voice.

I looked past her and saw that I now stood on a golden beach, with an ocean of cerulean blue stretching out before me. A copper sun warmed my skin and the sound of a child's laughter drifted from somewhere just out of sight.

Elena Grayloc slowly circled me, her fingertips trailing down the length of my arm.

I followed the movement, and the breath caught in my throat as I saw how smooth my skin had become. I lifted my hand, turning it over and marvelling at its flawless youth. My nails were cherry red, my palms supple.

Reaching up to my face, I ran my hand over my cheeks and neck.

Like my arm, the skin was taut and porcelain smooth as it had been in my youth.

'You're beautiful,' said Elena Grayloc, stepping back to admire my physique.

Only then did I realise I was naked, and one look down at my body revealed that all the ravages of age had been undone. Flesh that sagged from muscle was once again tight, the spots and blotches of age had vanished, and a strength flowed through me that I had not known in decades.

'Intoxicating, isn't it?' said Elena Grayloc, seeing my cheeks flush and my chest rise and fall with unbridled excitement. 'How swiftly we forget the vigour of youth. How easily we accept the decline of age and think it normal. But it doesn't have to be that way.'

The youthful energy filling my limbs and my heart and lungs was exhilarating. I felt the urge to wield this incredible power; to run, to fight, to couple with beautiful people until dawn crested the horizon. Such power was mine, had *always* been mine, but the passing of the years had stolen it from me without me even noticing.

No, it was worse than that. I had *let* it go.

I had foregone those pleasures of the flesh, denying my senses the experience of what it meant to be human. I looked back on the ascetic path my life had taken and felt a boiling wave of anger fill me.

'You can have it all again, Teresina,' said Elena Grayloc, stepping towards me and holding up a jagged shard of glass. I saw myself reflected in its silver depths, my once stern and lined face softened and young again.

The colour that had only recently begun to seep back into my hair was now fully restored. My lips were once again full, my cheekbones clearly defined and my eyes alive with the vitality and promise of youth.

'What is this...?' I said, and even my voice was renewed.

'It is *life*,' said Elena Grayloc. 'And it can be yours again. You have a mind of brilliance and flesh I can make whole again. If you let me...'

She reached out and placed her hands on my flat stomach. I felt motion stir within me, and gasped as the potential of new life fluttered in my once again fertile womb. My hand slipped protectively to the idea of a swelling in my belly, and tears pricked the corners of my eyes.

'Yes,' said Elena Grayloc. 'We will put that womb of yours to good use.'

I frowned at that, but she moved in close to me, and I forgot her presumption.

Her hands slipped around the small of my back, and my own hands laced themselves naturally around her neck. We stood facing one another like lovers.

We moved closer, but I could not say who was pulling who.

Elena Grayloc was beautiful in a way I had never experienced before. I wanted to know what she tasted like, how her skin felt upon mine. The scent of Fireblooms filled my senses and the heat of her skin was like a furnace on me.

I ran my hands through her hair, feeling the fused and melted shards of skull, the rubbery texture of overcooked meat under my fingertips. Fused brain matter and bone. Flash-boiled cranial fluids spilled over my hands.

I didn't care. I wanted to be with her, to lie upon the warm sand and let her sink into my flesh, to let her know me completely.

She felt my exploration of her shattered skull and said, 'The bastard killed me, you know.'

'Who?'

She ignored the question as her lips brushed against my ear. 'Came up behind me as I wrought destruction on His temple. Shot me in the back of the head and then threw me from the cliff. But you can make me whole again, Teresina. You can give me my life back'

'Anything,' I answered.

Something inside me was screaming, a silent prisoner with no voice in a cell with no window.

I knew I should listen to it, that what it was shrieking was vitally important, but the power surging through my rejuvenated flesh was too strong, and too desperate to cling to this rebirth.

'Let me in,' said Elena Grayloc. 'My body is too broken, its hurts too deep to heal. The cocoon of my *Inamorata* has sustained me, but its power is fading. You have a mind I yearn to inhabit, a body I *can* renew. A body I *have* renewed. You feel it already, don't you? The siren song of youth. It calls to you with all the promises of immortality, yes? Let me in and I will show you things you could never imagine, experiences you could never know.'

She leaned in and kissed me, and I felt the warmth of her tongue part my lips.

Its texture was rough, its wriggling motion pushing deeper into my throat.

I gagged as I tasted the reek of warm earth, the scratching texture of insect-like cilia as they wormed her tongue down my throat. The heat of Elena Grayloc's body changed from pleasurable warmth to a burning fire. I felt as though my flesh was slowly melting, becoming soft and malleable as she pressed herself against me.

The hardness of her fingers sank into the softness of my hips, pulling us together as though to press us into one body. I tried to resist, but her grip was locked to my flesh. Her tongue was no longer a tongue, but a writhing, frond-tipped proboscis that exuded a sickly sweet sap within me.

My stomach churned with motion, and again I felt the promise of new life. I felt the skin of my belly stretch as something new and living pulsed with sickening vitality, but this would be no innocent child, it would be a sickly parasite that would draw the life from me with every beat of its filthy heart.

My body could be young again, but would this be the price I must pay?

Not like this! Not like this!

Too often we look back on our lives and wish we could have our time again.

To do better, to do more, to walk the paths not taken.

But I have loved and I have learned. I have done my best to pass on my experiences to others. And in that I have no regrets.

In the end, I think that was what saved me.

Regret was what Elena Grayloc was counting on, a sense of my wasted potential that could be realised if I would only offer my flesh to her. And, yes, I sometimes thought of how the course of our lives would have been different had Teodoro and I chosen to have children, but I never once considered our choice to be a mistake.

But surrendering to Elena Grayloc would be the costliest mistake of my life.

She felt my resistance and her fury was terrible to

behold. She clung to my hips, her fingertips like hot pokers burrowing into the bone of my pelvis.

But my anger was the equal of her desire.

I dug my fingers into the shattered edges of her skull and pulled, furiously tearing chunks of hair-covered bone away.

She tried to pull back, but our lips were still locked together. I bit down on her proboscis tongue, sawing my teeth from side to side. The fleshy organ burst apart in my mouth, and I tasted warm fluid like stagnant swamp water. Rank clots of putrid blood made me gag as I now pushed her away.

I sank to my knees, bent double, and retched up a torrent of black pulsing *things* that burrowed into the sand to escape the glare of the sun's light. My stomach heaved again, disgorging a host of wet, slithering creatures like eyeless glossy eels.

My hands were bloody to the elbows, and I looked up at Elena Grayloc.

Not as she *wished* she had been.

But as she *was*.

In the blink of an eye, I was once again in the maze. Hammering sheets of rain drenched me to the bone. I was on my knees, holding sodden chunks of softened pink bone in my hands, from which hung thin wisps of silver hair.

Elena Grayloc loomed over me, her veil of glamours stripped away. The fleshy cocoon was draped around her like a shawl, and her broken body writhed in a final act of transformation. Violet light suffused her rippling flesh as it budded new limbs like pulsing tumours, extruded new organs and swelled with a power bolstered by what she had so very nearly stolen from me.

What I had so very nearly *given* her...

Her eyes were no longer rich gold-green, but a terrible, predatory neon-yellow.

'You could have had it all!' she shrieked, her face angular and daemonic. It was no longer human, yet possessed an alluring beauty that both repulsed and entranced my senses at the same time. I threw aside the gelatinous mass of brain and skull fragments clinging to my fingers and rose to face her.

'I do not want what you have to give,' I said, knowing she was going to kill me.

A succubus denied cannot allow those who reject it to live.

Her arms were slender, hooked things, her fingers no longer recognisable as human, but fused together like the claws of some mutant crustacean. She reached for me, ready to tear me apart, but then her head lifted and I saw a towering fury enter those coruscating eyes.

'You!' she shrieked. *'Faithless coward! Come to finish what you started?'*

I twisted my head and through tears of frustration and rainwater, I saw Kyrano enter the heart of the maze, the lasrifle still held at his chest. He lifted his hand and fastened his grip around the bronze plate covering the lower half of his face.

I had no idea what he was doing until I saw the servo-muscles grafted to his arm flex.

He pulled at the plate, slowly prising it from his skin.

Blood poured down his face as medical sutures and tissue grafts tore loose from their bone anchors. I saw the effort and agony it was taking Kyrano to tear it loose, his organic eye filled with furious determination.

Finally, the plate came loose in a welter of blood. It trailed an arc of viscous fluids, fused scraps of flesh and powdered bone fragments. A snaking length of rubber hose trailed from Kyrano's gullet, an oesophageal implant that was part rebreather, part digestive tract.

The servitor dropped the plate and ripped the tube from his throat. Yellowish stomach acid and intestinal fluids dribbled from its frayed end as he pulled it free. His exposed mouth was a ruin of splintered teeth and rotten gums. He shouted something with the tenor of a command, but its meaning was lost in a wet horror of bubbling blood and phlegm.

It was a death rattle and birth cry all in one.

I could not understand what he was saying or if what he was shouting were even words.

If they were, then they were the shrieks of a damned and tortured soul.

He shouted again, and this time I understood him.

Get down!

I dropped to the mud of the clearing as Kyrano shouldered the lasrifle and opened fire. A storm of blitzing las-fire filled the air, every bolt aimed with pinpoint accuracy. The servitor walked calmly forwards, the colonel's rifle blazing on full-auto.

Elena Grayloc came apart in an explosion of gore.

Half formed and melted bones exploded in the searing heat of the las-fire. Rotten meat vaporised in stinking clouds, and her monstrous limbs tumbled away as they were cut from her in the unending fusillade.

Eventually only a swaying trunk of bloodied meat remained.

Kyrano pumped shot after shot into Elena Grayloc's remains until the weapon ran dry, the powercell whining empty and the charging lever racked back against the breech.

Nothing remained that was recognisable as having once been human.

A lasrifle might not be the most powerful weapon in the Imperial arsenal, but at close range and in the hands of a skilled shooter it was devastating. Kyrano slung the rifle and spat a mouthful of black and oily phlegm at Elena Grayloc's vaporised corpse.

I had no real idea of the diabolical means by which she had sustained her life, but I felt sure nothing could survive such thorough destruction.

I rolled onto my haunches and squinted up through the rain.

Kyrano stood above me, a thick hand held out to me. His misshapen jaw struggled to form the shape of words.

'Am. Not. Servitor,' he said, and those three words told a horrifying narrative of cybernetically enforced slavery.

He hauled me to my feet, and I looked into his eye, now seeing life and soul filling the void behind it, a soul freed from what must have felt like an eternity in a lightless gulag.

'She did this to you,' I said, and he nodded. Perhaps it was the rain or perhaps he wept; I could not tell and would not shame him by asking.

I gestured towards the burnt ruin of flesh spread out in the mud.

'Is it over?' I asked.

Kyrano looked back to Grayloc Manor and shook his head.

'Not. Yet.'

We drove the Kiehlen 580 from the hangar and I watched through the rear window as Grayloc Manor burned. The storm had blown out with the colonel's death and the flames were eager to devour her ancestral home. Between us, we emptied two dozen canisters of promethium throughout its structure, taking particular care to ensure that every volume in the library would burn to ash.

Orange flames lit the night as we drove away from Vansen Falls, and I felt a particular symmetry had been achieved now that both promontories were home to fire-struck ruins.

I shall not fill these pages with the mundane details of the journey back to Servadac Magna, save to elaborate upon some gaps in my knowledge that Kyrano was able to fill.

Speaking was still difficult for him, for his transformation into cyborg had not been gentle, and the psychic blockers that had kept him mute and servile were akin to burning nails hammered into the centre of his brain. With Elena Grayloc's death, their intensity was waning, but it would take time for him to fully recover, if he ever would.

He told me of how he had seen Elena Grayloc on the

headland on the night of the previous storm, arms raised as if conducting its wrath. While her attention was fixed on whatever sorcery she was conducting, the agony of his burning nails had receded just enough for him to take the colonel's plasma pistol from the library and get close enough to her to put a single, overpowered shot through her skull. Such a wound ought to have killed her instantly, but her dark masters were not yet ready to release their mortal avatar.

Just as she re-established psychic control, Kyrano had kicked her from the cliff with his last independent thought. He had no knowledge of how she had come to be encased within the *Inamorata*, but it seemed clear to me that Garrett Grayloc was not the innocent I had feared when I killed him. I could only surmise that he had been a willing participant in his mother's scheme of rebirth. It was impossible to know for sure, but it was difficult to believe he had not been party to events at Grayloc Manor.

And the night I had woken to find Kyrano standing at my bed with what looked like a garrotte of twisted sheets in his hands? He had not been trying to kill me, he had been *saving* me. Elena Grayloc's malign influence permeated the entire house, and in her deathly, regenerative state, it seemed her mind roamed the site of her death with only fragmentary knowledge of what and who she was.

Seeing a stranger in her bed had likely stoked a murderous rage in her.

Kyrano had heard me choking and had rushed in to save me, and had in turn found himself the object of the colonel's psycho-kinetic fury.

Had the figure I had seen on the headland been a phantasm also conjured by her gestating nightmares? It was the only explanation I could think of, but who can know the minds of the mad or the designs of one fallen to the Ruinous Powers?

Who would wish to...?

I slept some of the way, exhaustion and the after-effects of adrenaline leaving me alternately weeping, angry, cold, terrified and determined.

The sun was cresting the horizon as the spires of Servadac Magna came into view.

'Where. To. Go. Now?' asked Kyrano, working his jaw from side to side.

I had given the matter careful consideration on the journey back.

Events at Grayloc Manor would eventually come to light. Investigators would find the corpse of Garrett Grayloc and perhaps they might even be able to positively identify him. It wouldn't take long to trace a line from him back to me, so we only had a short window in which to act.

Both books in the hidden study had been destroyed, but I remembered enough of what was contained in the ledger to know that the colonel's poisonous collection had spread far and wide. We would not be able to reach them all, but we could at least make a start.

'The Cardophian Repository,' I said.

And now we come full circle.

The candle is almost burned down, and this missive is complete. Now you know the truth of what happened at Grayloc Manor. Now you know the truth of the Dawn of Dark Suns.

I warned you that you would not thank me for these revelations.

Kyrano has almost finished his task, and the acrid reek of promethium fills the repository.

We spent the day gathering as much as we could fit onto an old cargo-8 and, using my access codes to the repository, which were still valid thanks to my regular consultations with the staff, entered and poured the flammable liquid wherever I could remember books of the colonel's being deposited.

I lament that I can see no other way to rid this world of Elena Grayloc's corruption, for who knows how far the malign power in her books has spread? It pains me to do this, for I have many fond memories of this building. But for all we know, every book on every shelf might be infected with the horrors Colonel Grayloc brought back from the howling darkness she found in the hostile void of space.

Nor are Kyrano and I exempt from this purge.

He lived with her taint in his mind for decades, and if I touch my hand to my belly, I fancy I can feel a tremor of movement. I cannot be certain, but the chance that Elena Grayloc was able to pass on something of her treachery into my flesh is too great a risk.

No, this must end tonight.

I look up and Kyrano nods. Our task is almost at an end.

I doubt this record will survive, for Kyrano is nothing if not thorough.

The truth of setting this down, then, is that it has only been for me.

Catharsis perhaps. Or maybe it is something more, something I cannot express but feel must somehow be recorded, even if the reasons for that are entirely selfish.

Once an archivist, always an archivist, I suppose.

Kyrano has lit the flare.

It burns so very bright.

So, too, shall we.[5]

5　　　Inquisitorial Note: The above confession was discovered in the burned ruins of the Cardophian Repository on Yervaunt. How it survived the fire that destroyed the rest of the building is a matter of some interest, as the murderer, Teresina Sullo, and her servitor accomplice were thorough in their application of flammable accelerants. How much of this record can be considered truthful is impossible to verify at this time, as both bodies found at the site bore signs of deep psychic manipulation. It is our recommendation that their remains be contained and transported securely to the nearest ordo facility for further psycho-forensic examination. We also recommend that this record be sealed to Omicron-level clearance and that investigations begin into Grayloc Trading Cartel. A last recommendation is that an interrogation be undertaken of the sole survivor of the campaign colloquially known as the Dawn of Dark Suns at the earliest opportunity. Ave Imperator!

ABOUT THE AUTHOR

Graham McNeill has written many Horus Heresy novels, including *The Crimson King, Vengeful Spirit* and his *New York Times* bestsellers *A Thousand Sons* and the novella *The Reflection Crack'd*, which featured in *The Primarchs* anthology. Graham's Ultramarines series, featuring Captain Uriel Ventris, is now six novels long, and has close links to his Iron Warriors stories, the novel *Storm of Iron* being a perennial favourite with Black Library fans. He has also written the Forges of Mars trilogy, featuring the Adeptus Mechanicus. For Warhammer, he has written the Warhammer Chronicles trilogy *The Legend of Sigmar*, the second volume of which won the 2010 David Gemmell Legend Award.

THE HOUSE OF NIGHT AND CHAIN
by David Annandale

At the edge of the city of Valgaast, Malveil awaits. It is a house of darkness, its halls filled with history and pain. It knows all secrets, and no weakness can escape its insidious gaze. Now it stirs eagerly at the approach of prey.

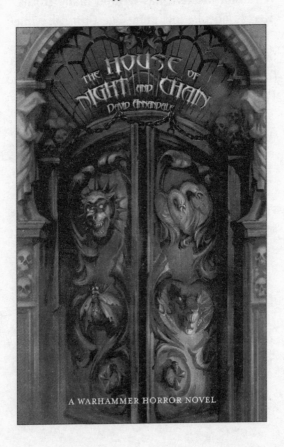

CHAPTER 1

Now

The antechamber to the Hall of Judgement on the battle-ship *Eternal Fury* was a semicircle, fifty-four paces across at its widest. I had counted. Against the fore wall, a single iron chair stood next to the heavy bronze doors that separated me from my judges. I had yet to sit in it. I could not keep still. I walked the periphery of the antechamber, finding no relief in movement, only the necessity to avoid the curse of stillness.

To port and starboard were deck-to-ceiling windows, and from the port one I could see the charred lump of coal that had been the world of Clostrum. The world it had been my duty to save. Every time I passed before that view, I paused, wincing through fresh spasms of guilt. Averting my gaze was not within my power. The sight pulled me, hooks sunk into my soul. Again and again, I stared at the dead world and then jerked away, my heart thumping hard, my gut dropping away, my left palm tingling with new sweat.

There was no feeling in my right palm. Nor anywhere else in my right arm, or my right leg. Or, more precisely, there was no natural feeling. They were my prosthetics, replacing the flesh and bone taken from me on Clostrum. I was not used to them yet. My pacing was more than restlessness. It was also my attempt to come to terms with the new realities of my body. The faint whirs of the servo-motors were still an alien sound, a machinic voice that I could not truly connect with myself. It was a whisper that followed me everywhere I went, its true source perpetually out of sight, though always near. The arm and the leg worked well, obeying the impulses sent by my brain. I did not consciously have to command their motions. At the same time, they were a strange land, a zone I did not recognise. They belonged to someone else, someone whose intentions perfectly reflected my own. I felt the phantom pains of my vanished limbs, and the aches corresponded to places on the prosthetics yet did not come from them. I was a divided being, playing at unity.

My soul was as split as my body. I was present in the moment, and grappling with the agony of my shame. I was also distant, part of my mind retreating into a cocoon of numbness, observing my torment with a cold disinterest.

I had been waiting in the antechamber for hours. When my eyes did not go to the ruin of Clostrum, they lingered on the relief sculpture of the bronze doors. On each was a massive figure, Justice personified in heroic lines, arms crossed, jaw stern, gaze directed far above my head, as if seeing the arrival of judgement. There was no mercy to be had here, no concessions.

I expected none. I desired none.

I did not think I desired anything. Not any longer. I awaited the call to pass through the doors with no impatience. I did not even feel the urge to get the process over with. There was only the shame, its spears battling with the protective shield of the numbness. The shield that held the memories of Clostrum at bay. I had to protect myself from them, or they would rip me apart. I would not be able to function at all. And if nothing else, I was determined to meet my fate with dignity. I owed that to my regiment. And to my fallen troops.

'Steady,' I whispered to myself as I approached the port window again. 'Steady.' But the effort to avoid the memories backfired. Instead of blocking them, I summoned them. They stormed my defences. They came for me with pincers and claws that could shred a Leman Russ like parchment. They came with bodies bloated with bioweapons. They came in a swarm that blotted out the sky and covered the land with an undulating carpet of horror. I saw the heroes of the Nightmarch, the soldiers who trusted me, who followed my commands without question, who looked to me for guidance and the path to victory. I saw the monsters turn them to blood and pulp. I saw the ocean of jaws devour my regiment.

I was in the roof hatch of my command Chimera again. The giant horror rushed us. It towered over the vehicle, its body armoured with impregnable chitin, its huge arms ending in talons like serrated spears. It stabbed its talons through the flanks of the Chimera, lifted it from the ground and ripped it in two. It hurled the halves away. I went flying and landed twenty yards from the burning wreckage. I tried to stand. I tried to make my *last* stand a worthy one. Before I could rise, the creatures were on me, marching over me, barely seeing me. One warrior form paused. Its talons pierced my shoulder and thigh.

The agony was fresh again. The agony and the sound, the awful tearing of muscle and the cracking of bone. The agony and the smell, the mix of my blood and the sharp, burning stench of xenos pheromones. The agony and the sudden absence, the *parting* of arm and leg from body.

And still other memories came, more fragmented but just as terrible, maybe even worse. They were confused impressions of gunfire, light and darkness, screams and roars. They were my last impressions as I wavered in and out of consciousness, of the troopers who came to my aid and died saving their failed colonel.

I hunched forward in the antechamber, clutching my false arm, my right leg feeling as if it were buckling, even though it could not. I gasped for air, and my nostrils were filled with the smell of xenos and massacre. My eyes watered. My chest heaved. I growled, because if I didn't, I would scream.

'Colonel, you may enter.'

The words jerked me from the memories. My eyes cleared. The bronze door had opened. Two men, one in the livery of the Imperial Navy, the other a surviving major of the Solus Nightmarch, stood on either side of the doorway.

I straightened up, cleared my throat and gave the major a curt nod. His name was Hetzer. He had been among those who had saved me. He was one of the few who had survived doing so.

I crossed the threshold into the Hall of Judgement. Four sculpted swords pointed to the centre of the vaulted ceiling, from which a great skull stared down. The room was circular, and I advanced down an aisle to its centre, to stand on a bronze aquila inlaid in the marble floor, directly beneath the gaze of the skull.

A ring of thrones surrounded me. All were occupied. The majority of the authorities present were of the Astra Militarum, most notably General Pereven of the Solus Nightmarch. There were a number of officers from the Imperial Navy as well, in deference to the fact that it was in their ship that this court was assembled. There were others too. There was Captain Numitor of the Ultramarines Eighth Company. I had never seen him before, but I knew who he must be. We had all known that the Ultramarines were fighting on Clostrum, though they had not been present near the battle I had lost. This was the first time I had been in close proximity to one of the Adeptus Astartes. I was dwarfed by his colossal stature. I felt something even worse than shame to be in the presence of so noble a warrior.

Sitting next to Pereven was a woman in solemn robes of black laced with gold. She was very old. The heavy chain and pendant of the Adeptus Terra seemed to weigh her neck down, but her eyes were piercing.

Pereven confirmed my surmise by introducing Numitor, and presented the woman as Lady Arrasq. 'The rest you know,' he said.

I did. I had the deepest respect for every officer in the room. It made my failure all the more painful to have it witnessed by them.

'Colonel Maeson Strock,' said Pereven, 'the Circle of Judgement has been called to consider your actions in the battle for Clostrum. Do you understand your position in these proceedings?'

'I do, sir.' I stood straight. I stared at a point on the wall just above the general's head. 'I understand that the work of the Circle is complete. Judgement has already been reached. I am here for it to be rendered, not to defend myself.'

'Good,' said Pereven. 'Before we pronounce the verdict, this court would like to hear your evaluation of the event.'

'Sir, I was charged with leading my regiment against the tyranid invasion and protecting the civilian population of Hive Throndhelm. I failed in this task. My regiment was defeated, taking severe losses, and Throndhelm was overrun. So was all of Clostrum. In the wake of the Imperial defeat, Exterminatus was declared. I make no excuses for the part I played in losing a forge world. Whatever the verdict of this court, I accept it with thanks and will do grateful penance.'

Pereven toyed with the stylus in his hands. 'Colonel, though you have described the events accurately, your analysis is incorrect.'

'Sir?' I asked, confused.

'You did not fail in your duty,' said Numitor. 'No success was possible, though none of us knew this at the outset of the battle.'

'You slowed the tyranids,' Pereven said. 'You bought enough time for a significant portion of the population of Hive Throndhelm to be evacuated off-world, along with a considerable amount of resources. Colonel, you are to be commended for your actions.'

'Commended,' I repeated softly. The word tasted like sawdust.

'Though Clostrum was lost,' said Numitor, 'the larger tyranid advance into this sector of the Imperium has been blunted, at least for now. You were part of a victory, colonel, not a defeat.'

The screams of devoured soldiers roiled in my memory, blotting out my sense of the chamber for a moment. If there was a triumph here, I could not find it.

'You fought hard,' said Pereven. 'You have done well, colonel.'

'Thank you, sir,' I managed. His praise struck my soul like a curse. 'I look forward to serving with honour wherever the Nightmarch is called to next.' It took a huge effort to utter those words. Sweat beaded on my forehead.

Pereven exchanged a glance with Arrasq.

'No,' said the noble who spoke for the Adeptus Terra.

'How much of the retreat do you remember?' Pereven asked before I could respond.

'Very little,' I admitted. 'I believe I was unconscious for most of it.'

'Despite your wounds, you were not. You continued to issue commands throughout.'

'Coherent ones?' I turned to look at Hetzer. He looked uncomfortable.

'Speak freely, major,' said Pereven. 'You will do no harm to your colonel. We already know the answer to his question. He does not, and he deserves the truth.'

Hetzer cleared his throat. 'No,' he told me. 'Many of your orders could not be followed.'

'Meaning you had the good judgement not to obey them,' I said sadly. 'Was I delirious from blood loss?' I asked Pereven.

'The medicae officers have concluded that this was only partly the case. You were suffering from other forms of shock, colonel.'

'You have given what you could to the battlefield, Colonel Strock,' Arrasq said. 'You have nothing left to give.'

What she said was true, and I knew it. Yet it felt like the most humiliating weakness to agree. Then she said, 'The Imperium still has need of your services.'

Hope flared. I was ready to agree to anything, as long as I could salvage even a thread of dignity. 'All I ask is to serve,' I said.

'Tell us about your home world, colonel,' said Arrasq.

I was puzzled, but did as she had asked. 'Solus is an agri world,' I said. 'Its seat of government is Valgaast, which is also its largest city. Its exports to the Imperium are on the order of twelve billion tonnes a year...' I trailed off, feeling foolish. 'I'm sorry, Lady Arrasq. I really don't understand what you want from me.'

'You have told me what I wanted to hear.' She glanced at the data-slate in her hands. 'Colonel, would you be surprised to learn that exports from Solus have been gradually falling for some time? And that the current level is just under ten billion tonnes a year?'

'I would be, yes, though it has been many years since I have had news from Solus. Have there been droughts?'

'Not of any unusual kind. The decline has been steady since the death of Leonel Strock.'

'My uncle was incapable of governing for the latter part of his life. That was why the regency was established.'

'Yes, and under your guidance the export levels were steady. In fact, they climbed. But not only is this no longer the case, evidence has also been uncovered of large quantities of Solus products entering black markets.'

I saw what Arrasq was implying. 'You believe the governing council has become corrupt.'

'We do. Its members are engaged in war profiteering on a large scale.'

'Leonel Strock died over thirty years ago. Has the problem been festering that long?'

'It has, but the council has been careful. The decline of exports and rise of profiteering were very gradual, unnoticeable from year to year. The wheels of the Administratum grind slowly. It is only recently that an audit of Solus' exports over the long term has been conducted.'

'The corruption will be deeply rooted, then.'

'Indeed. Until now, your duty to the Imperium has been on the battlefield, but matters have changed.'

'I am no longer useful in combat,' I said. I managed to keep the bitterness from my voice.

'This is your new campaign, colonel,' said Pereven.

'We believe it is only a matter of time before the council seeks to install a new lord-governor,' Arrasq went on. 'To date, it seems that the only barrier has been your hereditary claim. But that will not stop the council indefinitely. You must return, *Lord-Governor* Strock. Take up the title that is yours by right, and purge the council of corruption.' She paused. 'You must go home.' She watched me, gauging the effect of her words.

Home. I did not know if the word still had meaning. It had been so long. I was changed. Solus had changed too, in ways more profound and personal for me than the political situation.

Home. I pushed the word as far from my consciousness as I could. That was not far enough. It would come back for me all too soon. I would have to try to be ready for it.

I doubted I would be.

'Thank you, Lady Arrasq,' I said. I mouthed the correct responses. They sounded flat to me, as if a servitor were speaking instead of me. 'I am grateful for this assignment.' The word *redemption* rose in my thoughts. *Redemption for what? For which sin? Or maybe this is punishment. Perhaps this court is sentencing you without realising it.* 'I will return honour to Solus.'

'I'm sure you will, lord-governor.'

That was twice she had used the title. She was emphasising my new role. I was no longer to think of myself as a colonel in the Astra Militarum. I was returning to the other tradition of my family. I was a noble, and the duties were of a very different nature. She was also reminding me of the authority she represented. General Pereven and the other officers might control what happened to me within the aegis of the Nightmarch. It was not for them to declare me lord-governor. Even my family claim on the governorship did not, ultimately, rely on any authority on Solus. No matter how strong my right might appear in the traditions of my home world, those traditions were subject to the decisions that could, at any time, emanate from the Adeptus Terra. Arrasq could make or unmake me with a word.

I saluted Pereven, then turned, slowly, giving due acknowledgement to the full circle of my judges. They looked back at me impassively, expressions perfectly neutral.

Hetzer and the Navy officer opened the doors of the chamber for me.

What are you thinking? I wondered as I walked back down the aisle. I had been praised, not censured. But in every way that mattered, I was already no longer a colonel. *What do you see before you? Is that pity you are hiding? Is it gratitude that my fate is not yours? Is it contempt for my weakness?*

I was glad not to know. I had self-loathing enough to keep me occupied. No matter what I had been told, I despised the officer who had lost Hive Throndhelm. I hated the relief I felt in knowing I would not be returning to combat.

The echoes of screaming troops grew louder again. I managed to keep my breathing regular and my stride steady. I prayed to the Emperor for strength. I was terrified the memories would attack with all their monsters and shame me before I could leave the chamber.

I made it out with my dignity intact. I allowed myself to take a long, shuddering breath when I heard the doors close behind me. I kept walking, my action mechanical, as if all my limbs were prosthetic, and as if movement alone would get me away from the waking nightmares. I stopped in front of the port window. The dead planet turned slowly beneath the ship. It was free of nightmares, free of hope. It was nothing now. I was almost envious.

'I shall miss you, sir.'

I hadn't realised that Hetzer had followed me out. I did not jump. I took that as a small victory.

'Thank you, major.' I turned my back on the sight of Clostrum. 'Thank you for everything.'

His smile was crooked, skewed by the massive scar cutting across his face. He would bear the mark of saving his superior officer forever. 'It was an honour to serve with you.'

'The honour was mine. I thank the Emperor that you will continue to lead. I imagine these are your last days as major.'

He looked embarrassed. 'So I have been told,' he admitted.

'I am glad. Let me congratulate you and call you colonel now, before we part.'

We shook hands.

'I hope your return to Solus goes well,' Hetzer said.

I made myself smile. I wasn't sure that it could. I was

going home to mourning and to painful hope. I didn't know which was worse.

That night, I dreamt about the day I showed Malveil to my children. My vision of their deaths rose from the grave of memories and roared.

I woke with a gasp, and with the shrieks of lost comrades in my ears.

CHAPTER 2

The gate to Malveil was open when I arrived. I sat in the back of the car for a few moments after Belzhek, my chauffeur, had pulled over. The grounds were waiting, after so long, for me to claim them as the new lord of the manor. The last time I had seen Malveil, its sight had been tainted by my children's tears, and the stain lingered.

'Shall I drive in, lord-governor?' Belzhek asked. She was another veteran of the Nightmarch, mustered out by extensive injuries. She had been a sergeant, and her family was not wealthy, so her prosthetics gave her mobility but not much more. The lower half of her body was a platform with motorised treads. Her mechanism slotted well into the vehicle, but outside the car, she moved at a crawl. Her life was better than that of a servitor, but that was small reward for her service.

'No, thank you,' I said. 'I'll walk the rest of the way.' I wanted to feel the grounds as Malveil and I became properly acquainted for the first time. 'Wait here. I'll need you to take me to the Council Hall afterwards.'

'Yes, lord-governor.'

I got out of the car, shutting the door behind me with a hard clunk. The vehicle was an old one, as well maintained as it could be, though its engine grumbled loudly and the exhaust spewed blue smoke. It was a stolid thing, squat and heavy. It favoured strength over luxury, and I liked it. It sent the right signal about the kind of governor I intended to be.

I walked up to the gate, dwarfed by the ancient wall surrounding the estate. It was fifty feet high, a massive rockcrete barrier stained black with time. It had not had to defend Malveil against an attack for as long as the Strocks had owned the land, but when Leonel had turned into a recluse, it had held off the curious, the concerned and the scheming. The iron gate was just as high, each of its bars over a foot thick. I crossed the threshold into the land that was now mine and felt the strength of the wall at my back.

Let the council do its worst. Its corruption, no matter how thorough, suddenly seemed a weak thing indeed compared to the power that resided on this hill.

A gatehouse crouched against the interior of the wall, its gothic windows shadowed by its steeply gabled roof. It was the home of Rhen Karoff, the major-domo of Malveil. He had offered to meet me at the gate, but I had asked him to wait for me at the house itself. I needed the time alone to prepare myself. Things had changed since I had stood outside the gates with Eliana and the children. Hopes had died within its walls. This was not the return I had imagined for myself long ago.

But hopes were not reality. It was reality that I must face.

The route up the hill was barely a road. It twisted back and forth between the entrances to mines and quarries. The rockcrete had been broken up and rutted over the centuries by the passage of heavy machinery. The machines no longer travelled it. The mines were exhausted, Leonel had let the road fall further into disrepair, and nothing had been done to improve it since his death. I passed between gaping pits and dark tunnels burrowing into the bare stone of the hill. The mines were open graves. Here and there, the bones of cranes and excavators marked the tombs. The day was chilly, and a north wind, soft but insistent and steady, blew through the iron skeletons with a rusting, hollow whistle.

As I drew closer to the top of the hill, I left the remains of the mining behind. There were trees here, and they were all dead, killed by the toxins that had permeated the ground in the wake of the excavations. The Strock estate had been the source of our power, but the price had been the ruin of the grounds. There was no beauty in this land. It was grey and hard, a pitted fossil. And though the trees were dead, they refused to fall. They surrounded Malveil with their petrified death, branches reaching out to the leaden sky, splayed, angled, clutching, pleading.

The house had filled more and more of my vision

during my ascent. Sometimes it disappeared behind a mound of ejecta and then reappeared with greater force. The dead forest veiled it from view again, the tangles of branches and the crooked trunks concealing all but fragments of the house. Then I emerged from the trees, and it rose before me in its full power. I stopped, taking it in.

This is yours, now. This belongs to you.

I had trouble making myself believe that.

The Strocks belong to Malveil.

The thought was an odd one. I tried to dismiss it as unworthy fancy. It did not leave willingly, because it was confident in its truth, and it gnawed at my chest.

I tried another tactic. *All right, then. We belong to Malveil. It comes to the same. We are united in strength. Let me claim my birthright, and use it to save Solus.*